SAVAGE BLOOD

"Get up, white man," Iron Eagle said. "We are not finished."

Pike groaned as he rolled onto his stomach. Facing a large pile of tree branches used for firewood, he propped himself up on one of the smaller limbs. As he rose, he took hold of the wood and brought it around hard on the jaw of one of the braves in the lodge. On his feet now, he swung backhanded and connected with the head of the other Crow warrior next to Iron Eagle. Both men went down quickly onto the packed earthen floor.

Iron Eagle stepped up and grabbed his knife. "You are a worthy enemy, white man," the brave said, tensing for the attack.

"Like you said, chief. We ain't finished. Not by a long shot."

THE EXECUTIONER
by Don Pendleton

MOUNTAIN JACK PIKE

#4 CROW BAIT
JOSEPH MEEK

PINNACLE BOOKS
WINDSOR PUBLISHING CORP.

PINNACLE BOOKS

are published by

Windsor Publishing Corp.
475 Park Avenue South
New York, NY 10016

First printing: November, 1989

Printed in the United States of America

Prologue

I

The winter that year was particularly cold. On the Yellowstone River, it was frigid and unforgiving.

Jack Pike and Skins McConnell were camped for the night, a fire burning brightly between them, though neither looked into it, but rather across it. To stare into the flames would damage each man's night vision, and neither was willing to risk that, for the Yellowstone was home to the Blackfeet, the Crows, the Cheyennes, the Sioux, as well as others.

"Jesus," McConnell swore, "of all the winters I've spent in the mountains, this is the coldest."

Pike rubbed his hands together over the fire, staring at McConnell.

"The cold has never bothered me," he said, "but this cold is different. This must be like the cold one feels in death."

McConnell stared in turn at Pike and said, "That kind of talk brings nightmares, Pike."

The aim of Pike and McConnell was to hunt, for hunting on the Yellowstone, even in winter, was plentiful. There were elk and antelope, white-tailed deer and mule deer, but there were especially bison, which in the cold sought the shelter of the cottonwood groves. Pike and McConnell had two pack mules piled high with meat and skins. In the cold the meat did not spoil as quickly as it might have. Over the fire now they cooked and ate, warming their insides with the meat and with coffee.

"I sure wish we'd brought a couple of squaws along for warmth," McConnell said.

"We talked about that."

"I know we did."

"You lie down with a squaw and the next morning you don't want to get up and hunt."

"I know, I know," McConnell said, "but right now lying with a squaw is on my mind more than hunting is."

"You want to call this hunting trip off?" Pike asked.

"No, no," McConnell said, "I ain't sayin' that."

"Then what are you saying?"

McConnell looked at his friend and said, "I'm sayin' I'm cold, that's what I'm sayin'. Ain't nothing more to it than that."

"We'll move toward Clark's Fork tomorrow," Pike said. "We can sit there and the game will come walking right up to us."

"What fun is there in that?" McConnell said.

"The fun comes later, after we've sold everything and have our pockets filled with money."

McConnell poured himself another cup of coffee, even though he knew it would do no good. When you drank the coffee it warmed you, like a tease, but soon enough the warmth was gone and the cold was back.

"Sometimes I wonder . . ." he said.

"Sometimes you wonder what?" Pike asked.

"Even filling your pockets with money doesn't last forever," McConnell said. "Before you know it, the money's gone and you're scrambling for more."

"Well then, why don't you save some of your money?" Pike asked.

McConnell looked at Pike like he was crazy and said, "Now where's the fun in *that?*"

In the morning they rose a little after the sun did. Naked, Pike washed with ice he melted in a pot over the fire, enjoying the way the cold bit at his wet skin, and the way the sun warmed it. He would have preferred to wade into the river, but at the moment it was frozen solid.

"I don't know how you can do that," McConnell said as Pike emptied out the water, which was dripping off his beard and mustache.

McConnell was in the act of relieving himself on the cold ground, and steam was rising from his piss.

"Thick skin," Pike said, shaking his head so that beads of water flew this way and that.

"I been meaning to talk to you about this."

"This what?"

"Bathing."

"What about it?"

"You did it a lot."

"So?"

"So . . . it ain't natural."

"For who?"

"For *anybody.*"

"You take care of your body your way and I'll take care of mine my way," Pike said, reaching for his britches.

While Pike was washing McConnell had put the coffee on and he handed Pike a cup.

"Thanks."

Pike lifted the cup to his mouth and then stopped short, staring over the rim of the cup.

"What is it?" McConnell asked.

7

"Company."

McConnell turned and looked in the same direction and saw what Pike saw.

Indians, two of them.

"Crow," Pike said.

"Blackfeet," McConnell said, at the same time.

"I know a Crow when I see one, Skins," Pike said, "and now I see two."

"Well, I see two Blackfeet," McConnell said, stubbornly.

"Whatever they are," Pike said, "should we invite them for breakfast?"

"I think we should skip breakfast," McConnell said. "What do you say?"

Pike took one sip of the coffee and then dumped it out on the frozen ground, causing steam to rise from it.

"I'm with you."

McConnell emptied the coffee pot and hurriedly stowed it away. They saddled their horses and loaded the mules, trying to seem as if they weren't in a hurry.

"I wonder what attracted them to us?" Pike asked as they mounted up.

"They probably never seen a naked white man as big as you before," McConnell said. "I told you that bathing stuff was unnatural."

"More likely they're upwind of us and they smelled you," Pike said.

"Wonder how many of them are following these two bucks," McConnell said.

"I don't know," Pike said, "but it's sure to be more than I want to try and handle."

"Maybe they won't attack us?"

"Crow or Blackfeet," Pike said, "with the way we got these two pack mules piled high, I don't think they're gonna be able to help themselves."

McConnell shivered, from more than just the cold.

"I think you're right," he said.

"Let's just get a move on and see how much space we can put between us and these two bucks," Pike suggested.

"One thing's sure," McConnell said.

"What's that?"

"We sure as hell ain't gonna be able to outrun 'em."

They rode for half the day and didn't put a dent in the space between them and the two Indians who were following them.

"They can close on us at any time," McConnell said.

"Sure can."

"We've got to put some distance between us and them, Pike."

"There's another way we can go," Pike said.

"What's that?"

"We can get rid of them."

"Kill 'em?"

Pike nodded.

"Ain't that askin' for trouble?"

"I don't believe we have to ask for it, Skins," Pike said. "I think it's found us all by itself."

McConnell considered that and said, "You might be right. How do we do it?"

"As soon as we're out of their sight for a minute I'll slip down from my horse and wait for them. You keep on going."

"Right."

Soon enough they come to an outcropping of rock that shielded them from the sight of the Indians. Pike, knife in one hand and Kentucky pistol in the other, slid from the saddle and scrambled up onto the rock. McConnell took the reins of Pike's horse and continued to lead it and the pack animals on.

Pike waited patiently. He was holding his pistol, but

he knew he wasn't about to use it. Not without knowing how far behind them the main body of Indians was. He'd take care of one brave with the knife, and use the pistol as a club on the other one.

Finally the two braves came around the bend, sitting their ponies high and looking straight ahead of them. Pike let them get a little ahead of him, and then dropped down on them from behind. He landed between them and took them both from their saddles.

With the element of surprise on his side he was able to dispatch one brave quite easily by cutting his throat. The other brave, however, was quicker to recover and rolled away from Pike, producing his own knife.

Pike got to his feet and faced the brave, who was smaller than he was, but sturdily built. He held his knife in his right hand, blade up, and waited for the brave to make the first move.

The white man had more patience than the red, and the Indian finally sprang forward, his blade flashing in the sunlight. Pike brought his knife up to parry the Indian's blade, and then brought his left hand around. The butt of his Kentucky pistol slammed against the side of the Indian's head and the brave went down in a heap. Pike leaned over the Indian, prepared to kill him, but had a second thought. Perhaps finding one dead and one alive would confuse the others, forcing them to stop and ponder a course of action. Two dead braves would leave them no alternative, but one and one might give them pause.

Pike turned as Skins returned, leading Pike's horse, but without the pack animals.

"Tied them off up ahead," he said, handing Pike his reins.

Pike mounted up and they both looked down at the braves.

"I told you they were Crows," Pike said.

McConnell grunted and said grudgingly, "Well, they *looked* like Blackfeet."

II

It was early the following day that they discovered that Pike's ploy had not worked the way they had hoped.

Apparently, the main war party of Crows had split in two, one half continuing on their trail and the other half taking a shortcut and getting around in front of them.

"We're in a squeeze, Pike," McConnell said. "Six in front, and six behind. We'll have to stand and fight."

"We got some time before they reach us," Pike said. "We've got one other chance."

"What's that?"

"Cross the ice to the other side of the river."

"With these spraddle-legged mules? They'd never make it."

"We could leave the mules behind. The Crows would love that."

"All of our work to get this stuff and you want to leave it all behind?" McConnell said. "I'd rather die fighting."

"You got another idea?"

McConnell stared at the frozen Yellowstone and then said, "Yeah, I do. Give me your blankets."

"Blankets?"

"Come on, don't argue."

Pike handed down his two blankets and McConnell dismounted and took down his own blankets, then gave Pike his horse's reins.

"Go on across!" he said.

"Skins—"

"Move! We ain't got much time!"

Pike, realizing there was no time to argue, decided to trust his friend. He moved onto the ice with his horse, trailing McConnell's, and walked over the ice to the bank on the other side. When he got there he turned his horse around and couldn't believe what he saw.

McConnell had set their blankets down end to end on the ice and was walking the mules over them! The animals were moving slowly, but they were moving.

One time McConnell had to leave the mules, run back, move the blankets around in front of them again and then lead them on until they were on the bank with Pike.

"Skins," Pike said, handing his friend the reins to his horse and accepting his blankets back, "that was purely brilliant."

Fuses popped from the other side as the Crows reached the bank.

"Pat me on the back another time," McConnell said, mounting up. "Let's get out of here."

As they rode away the Crows glared after them, wondering how the white men had managed to get across the ice with two mules!

Just on the off chance that magic might have been involved, the war party decided not to follow.

Part One
Winter Quarters

Chapter One

Jim Bridger was wintering that year on the banks of the Yellowstone River with 240 men, most of whom were hunters and trappers. There were women among them—wives and squaws—and some of the men and women were simply camp keepers.

The joy of winter quarters was that the man had little to do but gather cottonwood bark for their horses, hunt game, and eat what the camp keepers cooked for them.

Bridger knew that both the Crows and the Blackfeet frequented the area, and if they weren't fighting each other they were likely to attack the whites. He kept a guard out day and night, because he felt that as long as they were constantly alert, the Indians would not attack them. If they could have been taken by surprise, they might have been attacked already.

A hunting party came back into the camp and Bridger went to meet them. It was his custom to check with each party as to what sign they might have seen of Indians.

Bridger was surprised to see two strangers riding into camp with the party—and then even more surprised when he recognized the two men.

Although several days had passed since crossing the

ice, Pike and McConnell kept a wary eye ahead *and* behind them, and alternated watches at night. After all, although they had left a Crow war party behind, there were still other war parties they could have run into.

Well, they finally ran into another party, but it was not a war party of Indians, but a hunting party of whites.

"Hold up," Pike said.

"What?" McConnell asked.

"I hear something coming this way."

They both remained silent and listened and, sure enough, they both heard the sound of approaching horses, and the murmur of voices.

"Now what?" McConnell asked, unsheathing his rifle.

"Easy," Pike said. "I don't think they're Indians."

"Why not?"

"Listen, Skins," Pike said.

For one thing the sounds the horses were making indicated that they were shod, and not unshod Indian ponies. For another, although they couldn't clearly make out what was being said, the voices did sound as if they were speaking English.

"Let's just hold our ground and see what develops," Pike said.

McConnell nodded nervously, hoping that his friend was right.

After a few moments the first rider came into view and was obviously white. He was bundled up against the cold, of course, but there was no mistaking the white face and long beard.

As the other hunters came into view behind the lead rider, McConnell breathed a sigh of relief and he and Pike moved forward to meet with them.

"Hello, there," Pike called.

"Hello," the others called.

As they reached each other Pike reached to grasp

the lead man's hand in a friendly handshake.

"We're glad to see you," Pike said. "We're hunting the area and had a run-in with a Crow war party."

"We're wintering near the Yellowstone," the man said, "and we were out doing some hunting."

"Looks like you did well," McConnell said, looking at the pack animals who were hauling the fruits of the hunt, both antelope and buffalo meat, and some skins.

"It may be cold," the man said, "but the hunting is fine. It looks as if you've done pretty well, yourself."

"We were doing fine before we ran into those Crow warriors," McConnell said.

"Who is your booshway?" Pike asked.

"Jim Bridger."

Pike and McConnell exchanged a glance.

"I didn't know Bridger would be wintering in this area," Pike said.

"You know Bridger?"

"Are you kidding?" McConnell asked. "This is Jack Pike, friend. He and Bridger are good friends."

"I know Bridger," Pike said.

"Jack Pike, eh?" the spokesman said. "Well, my name's John Candy, and I'm pleased to make your acquaintance, Pike."

"Same here, Candy. Meet Skins McConnell."

McConnell leaned across and shook hands with John Candy.

"Are you heading back to your camp?" Pike asked.

"We are, for sure. We'd be pleased to have you come back and eat with us. I'm sure Bridger will be glad to see you."

"Sounds good to me," McConnell said. "How many men you have in camp?"

"Better than two hundred."

"That should dissuade a war party," McConnell said.

"A small one, anyway," Pike said. "You lead the way,

Candy, and we're with you."

"Jack Pike!" Jim Bridger said. He stood with his hands on his hips and waited for Pike, McConnell, and John Candy to reach him.

"Found these two wandering around out there, Bridger," Candy said. "Claim they know you."

"Oh, they know me, all right," Bridger said, "and I know them."

Pike dismounted and clasped hands with Bridger. Others in camp stopped what they were doing to watch the two big men shake hands.

"What are you doing out here?" Bridger asked.

"Hunting," Pike said, "and dodging Crow war parties."

"Hello, Skins," Bridger said, shaking hands with McConnell.

"Well, you fellas won't have to worry about any small war parties while you're with us," Bridger assured them. He looked at Candy and said, "Did you ask these two to join us for dinner?"

"I sure did."

"Well, I guess we'll have to feed them, then," Bridger said. "You fellas want to get warmed up in my tent?"

"We wouldn't mind," McConnell said.

"Candy, why don't you see to their stock? I'll take them over to my camp."

"Right."

Bridger led Pike and McConnell to his tent but instead of going inside they sat at a fire that Bridger had going right outside.

"Tell me about this set-to you had with the Crow," Bridger said.

Pike told him all about it and ended by explaining the way McConnell had gotten the two mules across the ice.

Bridger was laughing hard by the time Pike finished

his story.

"Well, hell, Skins," Bridger said, "those Crow must have spit fire. I'll bet they couldn't figure how you got them mules across."

"It was just something that came to me," McConnell said, somewhat sheepishly.

"Well, don't be so damned modest, Skins," Bridger said. "It was inspired."

"Yeah, it was," Pike said, slapping his friend on the back.

"Okay," McConnell said, shrugging, "it was."

Candy and another man came over with some food and coffee for Bridger, Pike, and McConnell, and Bridger then asked Candy to sit and join them.

John Candy was almost as big as Pike and had very dark black hair and beard. He sat down with a plate of meat and beans and listened while Pike and Bridger did some reminiscing about the last few times they had crossed trails.

"You fellas sound as if you've had some pretty high times," Candy said.

Pike looked closely at Candy, whose hat was tied down with a scarf, and realized that this was a young man, at twenty-five or so easily ten years younger than the three of them.

"We've had some good times . . ." Pike said.

"And some bad ones . . ." Bridger added.

"What are you having now, Jim?" Pike asked.

"Well, we've been here about a month now and the hunting is plentiful," Bridger said.

"What about the Indians?" McConnell said.

"We haven't had any trouble with them so far," Bridger said. "I think I've got them confused."

"How so?" Pike asked.

"Well, I'm not letting them get a good look at just how many men I've got here," Bridger explained. "I don't think anyone—the Blackfeet, the Crow, or *anyone*—will come in on us without knowing what our

17

strength is."

"Good point," Pike said.

"As long as we can keep them guessing I think we're safe," Bridger said.

"And what happens when they finally make their guess and come in?" McConnell asked.

"Well, we've got plenty of men and more than enough powder to more than hold our own," Bridger said. "I didn't plan this lightly."

"Knowing you," Pike said, "I'm sure you didn't."

"John, have we got accommodations for these two?"

"I don't know, Jim," Candy said. "but I'll check." He put his plate down and went to do just that.

"Is he your second?" Pike asked.

"He is."

"A little young, isn't he?"

"He's bright, he listens, and he's a fast learner," Bridger said.

"This is a new role for you, isn't it?" Pike asked, smiling.

"What role?"

"Teacher?"

"I'm just trying to make sure he knows how to survive, that's all," Bridger said.

"Well, if he listens to you, he'll learn, all right," McConnell said.

"How long you two plan on staying with us?" Bridger asked.

"Well, since we didn't know you were in the area, I guess we don't rightly know how to answer that," Pike replied.

"Well, we can talk about that in the morning."

Candy returned at that moment and said, "We found a place for them, Jim."

"Good," Bridger said, standing. Pike and McConnell followed his example. "Get some rest, boys. Tomorrow we can talk about your immediate plans."

"It's good to see you again, Jim," Pike said, shaking

hands with Bridger again.

"Don't know who I'd rather run into unexpectedly, Pike," Bridger said.

Pike and McConnell moved away from the tent and Bridger took hold of Candy's arm, delaying him for a moment so he could speak to him.

"You do something about keeping them warm tonight?" he asked.

"Don't worry, Jim," Candy said knowingly, "they won't freeze."

"Good," Bridger said. "Maybe we can convince them to stay on with us. Can't think of two extra guns I'd rather have, John, especially Pike."

"I've heard a lot about him, Jim," Candy said. "Is it all true?"

"All true, lad," Bridger said, "and more, much, much, more."

Candy nodded and went to show Pike and McConnell to their quarters.

John Candy had been pleased and delighted when Jim Bridger chose him to come along to winter on the Yellowstone. Bridger was a legend in the mountains, and Candy had jumped at the chance to learn from a legend. He had never expected to be able to observe two legends at the same time.

He hoped Pike would agree to stay, even if it was for a short while.

Chapter Two

"I hope you fellas don't mind sharing a tent," Candy said.

"That's no problem," Pike said, "we've shared quarters before."

"No," Candy said, "I don't mean with each other." Candy stopped and said, "Skins, you'll be sleeping here."

McConnell looked at Pike and shrugged.

"Okay, thanks, John," McConnell said, and went inside the tent.

"Your tent is this way," Candy said to Pike.

Pike followed Candy farther down, past two or three other tents and leantos until the younger man stopped in front of a small tent.

"This one's yours," Candy said. "Sorry it's not bigger, but once you get inside I don't think you'll mind."

"It's fine."

"Look, Pike," Candy said, "I know Bridger is gonna talk to you about this tomorrow but I'd really like it if you agreed to stay on with us for a while."

Pike studied the younger man for a moment, then decided that he wouldn't ask him why. That was pretty much self-explanatory. The kid was going to Rocky Mountain College here, and he was looking for another teacher.

"We'll talk about it tomorrow," Pike said.

"Sure, sure," Candy said. "Listen, your gear is already in there."

"Thanks."

"Enjoy your night, eh? Keep warm."

Keep warm, Pike thought as he ducked into the tent. What the hell kind of advice was that in this weather? Did he need to be told that?

The inside of the tent was cold, but it was nothing compared to the weather outside. He immediately felt the difference as he entered. Without the wind the cold didn't seem as biting.

There was a lamp lit inside and by it he saw that someone was lying on the floor on top of some blankets.

He squinted, trying to make the form out. When she sat up he saw that it was a woman. She had long dark hair, dark skin and a wide, full-lipped mouth. As her lips parted tentatively, he saw a flash of white teeth.

Now he knew what Candy had meant by enjoy his night and keep warm. They had furnished him with a squaw.

Some of the men in camp, he knew, would have their wives with them for warmth and comfort. The other men would share some of the other women — both white and Indian — who had come along to keep the camp, and supply warmth and companionship when it was needed.

"I am called Jeanna," she said.

"Hello, Jeanna."

"You are Pike?"

"I am."

"I am for you tonight, Pike," she said, "and for as long as you stay."

She was sitting on a double thickness of blankets, and had a third wrapped around her. In a corner Pike saw his own two blankets, probably dry now after lying on the ice.

22

"Look, Jeanna," he said, "I've got two blankets that can keep me very warm tonight. You really don't have to do this."

"It is why I am here."

"Yeah, I know, but—"

"Blankets can keep you warm," she said, "but they cannot give you what I can give you."

With that, she opened the blanket and let it drop from her shoulders. Pike saw that she had a fine body with big, firm breasts and broad shoulders. Standing she would probably be almost five foot eight. Her nipples were already tightening, either from desire, or from the cold.

"Come," she said, spreading the blanket wide. He could see the dark hair at the shadowy juncture of her thighs. "Come and keep warm."

Jesus, he thought, why not? He undid his britches and slid them off, gathered up his two blankets and joined her on hers.

They wrapped themselves up and she helped him slip out of his coat and shirt. Her bare skin was burning, warming him instantly. Her hands reached between them to grasp his penis, which was now raging and huge.

"Oh . . ." she said, closing her eyes and squeezing him.

He slid down so he could run his mouth over her breasts, sucking the nipples, which were almost as thick as the tips of his thumbs. She moaned as he suckled them and she slid one hand down to cup his testicles.

She put her face against his neck and said, "Can you get this from a blanket." Her breath was hot.

"No," he had to admit, "I surely couldn't . . ."

He wondered idly if McConnell were facing the same, er, situation . . .

Skins McConnell wasn't shocked that the woman waiting for him in his tent was white. Well, actually it was probably her tent. He knew that trappers and hunters brought mostly squaws with them, but once in a while there were some white women along, some of them simply looking for a place to stay. Others were white women who had been taken by the Indians at some point in their lives, and who were actually more Indian than white.

This woman must have been very popular with the Indians because she was blonde, and Indians didn't often see blonde women with skin as white as this one had.

"Surprised?" she had asked.

"At what?"

"That I'm white?"

"No," he'd said, "I'm not surprised."

"I just needed someplace to spend the winter," she'd started to explain.

"You don't have to explain to me," he'd told her, gathering her into his arms . . .

McConnell had not been quite as hard to convince as Pike had been. Maybe that was because it had been a while since he had seen a blonde woman.

He slid into the blankets with her, his hands roaming her body. She had small breasts with large nipples, and the hair between her legs was light, like down. Wrapped in the blankets the way they were he couldn't see it, but he knew it would be the same fine blonde as the hair on her head.

They had coupled eagerly, and McConnell knew that the eagerness was genuine on her part. He didn't know about her, but he didn't care much. Even if she was only fulfilling her function, she was doing a damned good job of it . . .

"Would you like some coffee?" Jeanna asked.

"I wouldn't mind," Pike said, "but that would mean you'd have to get dressed and go out into the cold."

She sat up and shrugged off her blanket, standing up. He'd been right about her height. Standing in the dim light of the storm lamp she looked like acres of woman flesh, big breasts and hips, long legs, chunky ass.

"The cold doesn't bother me," she said, smiling. "I will get you some, and add some whiskey to it."

"Fine."

He watched with pleasure as she got dressed, her breasts swaying and tapping lightly together as she bent over to put on her moccasins.

"I will be right back," she said.

"I'll wait here," he promised.

He lay back, the blankets held all the way up to his neck. Her warmth was still inside and he didn't want any of it to escape.

He wondered idly if she was Crow or Blackfoot.

Chapter Three

Pike and McConnell spent a more comfortable night than they had in some time. Pike remembered what he had told McConnell about taking a squaw along with them. Lying next to Jeanna, feeling her warm flesh against his, he knew he had been right. Even now he wanted nothing more than to just stay where he was for as long as he could—maybe even until winter passed.

He moved away from her and tried to disentangle himself from the blankets without waking her. Naturally, it couldn't be done. She woke and stretched, her arms reaching beyond the blankets, causing them to slip down so that he could see her big breasts flattened out against her chest. He leaned over and licked each nipple until it hardened, and she reached up and laced her fingers behind his neck.

"You are the gentlest lover I have ever been with," she whispered to him. "That is surprising, especially in a man who is so big."

He kissed her, tweaking one of her nipples and said, "You're easy to be gentle with, Jeanna."

He started to rise but she wouldn't release him.

"Jeanna," he said, and she reluctantly let him go.

He stood up, naked, and drywashed his face.

"The cold is not your enemy, either, is it?" she asked.

"Not exactly," he said. "I wouldn't want to walk around in it for hours, but in the morning it wakes me up."

She sat up and asked, "Is there something I can get you?"

"Yes," he said, "a basin of water and a cup of coffee."

"I will get it."

She stood up and dressed quickly, in a buckskin top and leggings.

While he waited for her to return he pulled on his britches and his boots. Although he didn't dislike the cold, the winter meant he had to wear boots instead of moccasins. *That* he didn't like.

Jeanna returned, carrying a basin of water in one hand and a cup of steaming coffee in the other.

Pike took the coffee and asked, "What time is it?"

"The sun has been up for about a half an hour," she said.

"Is the camp awake?"

"Most of it," she said, "but we all have instructions. We have certain times when we are not supposed to walk around."

That had to be part of Bridger's plan to keep the Indians guessing about their numbers. Pike knew that he would have worked it in three shifts, so that the best guess anyone could make would be about eight men. Anyone acting on that guess would find a rude welcome awaiting them if they acted on it.

Pike sipped the coffee while it was still steaming and then washed his face and torso with the water. Instead of putting his shirt on right away he let the water dry by itself, enjoying the cold on his chest and the heat of the coffee on his insides.

Finally, he pulled his shirt on, followed by his coat.

"What shift are you on?" he asked.

"The women may move about at will," Jeanna said. "It is the men who must abide by the schedule."

"I wonder what my schedule is?"

"There are certain men — Bridger, Candy, and some others — who are free to move around at any time. As guests, I would say you and your friend would also be able to do so."

"Is my friend up yet?"

She smiled with genuine mirth and said, "Your friend is with Donna. I do not think he will be out and about for some time."

"Who is Donna?"

"A white woman who was taken by the Blackfeet when she was very young," Jeanna said. "She was rescued by whites four years ago, and has been showing her appreciation ever since."

"And you, Jeanna?" he asked. "Who are your people? Crow?"

"I spit on Crow *and* Blackfoot. I am Nez Perce," she said, proudly.

He finished the coffee and she offered to get him another cup.

"No, I'll get it myself," he said, standing up. He took the basin so he could empty it out.

"I must go and help prepare breakfast for the camp," she said.

As they started out of the tent she touched his arm and asked, "Will you be staying?"

He looked down at her and said, "I don't know, Jeanna. I have to talk to my friend."

She smiled.

"What are you smiling at?"

"If Donna has anything to say about it, you will be staying."

He laughed now and said, "Don't tell me my friend got the best part of this deal because he ended up with Donna and I ended up with you?"

She gave him a different kind of smile and said, "You do not believe that."

"No," he said, "I guess I don't."

Pike and Jeanna separated outside the tent and Pike walked toward Bridger's tent. On the way he was passing the tent where McConnell spent the night when his friend stepped outside and pulled up short when he saw Pike.

"Oh, it's you."

"How was your night?"

McConnell squinted at Pike and asked, "Was there a girl waiting for you last night?"

"Yes," Pike said, "and you?"

"Oh, yeah," McConnell said. "My legs feel so weak I can hardly walk, Pike. I swear, I never met a woman who liked it so much."

"Too much for you, eh?" Pike said, smiling.

"Hell, no," McConnell said, indignantly, "I'm just a little out of practice, is all."

"How about some coffee?"

"I could use it."

Together they walked toward Bridger's tent. They could see the fire still going out front, and a pot of coffee on it.

"Uh, what are we gonna do?" McConnell asked.

"About what?"

"I mean, are we gonna stay here a while, or move on?"

"Well," Pike said, "we're supposed to be hunting."

"I know that," McConnell said, "but we can hunt and stay here at the same time."

Pike looked at his friend and said, "I see Jeanna was right."

"Who's Jeanna?"

"A young lady I met last night," Pike said. "She said that Donna would make you want to stay."

"Oh yeah," McConnell asked, "well I don't hear you complaining about how you spent your night."

"I don't have any complaints," Pike said, "but I sure don't want to stay here all winter, Skins. You know I like to move around."

"I know that, Pike."

"You could stay, though," Pike said. "It ain't written in stone that you have to go where I go."

"Well, I know that, too, but we started this trip together, didn't we? Ain't we always finished what we started together?"

"I guess so."

"Besides," McConnell said, "I didn't say anything about staying here *all* winter."

"Well," Pike said, "I guess we could stay for a little while. A few days, maybe a week."

"Sure," McConnell said, "we can rest up for the rest of our hunting trip."

"We can talk to Bridger about it," Pike said, "see if he's got room for us."

"Hey, it ain't like we've got nothing to toss into the pot," McConnell said. "We've got meat, and skins, and we got our rifles. I think Bridger would be more than glad to have us."

"There he is coming out of his tent now," Pike said to his friend, "so why don't we just ask him, huh?"

"So," Bridger called out to them, "did you fellas manage to keep warm last night?"

He began to pour out some coffee and handed them each a cup when they reached him. They sat around the fire together.

"That was a dirty trick, Jim," Pike said.

"What trick?" McConnell asked.

"I was only trying to give you a little incentive to stay on," Bridger said to Pike.

"Stay on?" McConnell asked. "You mean you want us to stay on?"

"Of course I do," Bridger said. "You two are worth any ten men I already have with me."

"And, of course, you know McConnell's weakness

for warm blondes," Pike said. He looked at his friend and said; "Donna is a blonde, isn't she?"

"That she is," McConnell said, still a bit confused.

"And I'll wager she was warm enough."

McConnell nodded.

"And your woman, Pike?" Bridger asked. "Was she warm enough?"

"Like this fire," Pike said.

"Then you'll stay on?"

"For a week, maybe," Pike said, "just to rest up."

"A week?" Bridger said, teasingly. "Maybe more?"

Pike locked eyes with his friend and then nodded, saying, "Maybe more."

"Ah ha, I knew it," Bridger said. He reached over and slapped Pike on the knee heartily. "Come on, lad, let's get you some breakfast. When you see how well we eat you'll stay until winter is gone."

McConnell rose and followed Bridger toward breakfast. Donna had been blonde and warm, but she had also helped him work up an appetite.

Pike poured the remnants of his coffee into the fire, causing it to flare briefly, and then rose and followed Bridger and McConnell.

A week, he thought, maybe more . . . but not a whole damn lot more!

Chapter Four

The Crow chieftain called "The Bold" sat in his lodge, thinking about the white men camped down by the river.

As long as he and his braves had been watching the white man's camp, they still had not been able to determine how many men were there.

"The Bold" did not want to lead his men into battle without knowing what they were facing. True, one Crow was worth any five white men, but as the leader of his people he still wanted to know what he was facing.

Iron Eagle entered his lodge and waited for "The Bold" to speak.

"Take four braves and go to the river," the chieftain said.

"Again?"

"And why not?"

"Why do we not just kill them," Iron Eagle said, "kill them all?"

"All?" his leader asked.

"Yes, all of them."

"And how many is all, Iron Eagle? Tell me that, eh?" the chief asked.

"All?" Iron Eagle said. "I do not know how many they are."

"Then how many braves will it take to kill them all,

eh?"

"I — I do not know."

"Then go," the chief said. "Take as many men as you think you need and go, kill them all — or be killed. It's your choice."

Iron Eagle, a young man — more than twenty years younger than "The Bold," — tall and strong, stared at the old man for a few seconds, and then said, "I will take four men."

"Look long and hard, Iron Eagle," the other man said. "We need to know how many."

"As you say, my Chief."

"And if you can catch any of the men alone, capture him. If we can capture a man, we can torture the information out of him. He will tell us how many they number."

"If it takes the passing of ten moons or more, I will capture one of them."

"Yes," the chief said, "and then we will know how many they are, and how many we will kill."

"All of them," Iron Eagle said.

"Yes," "The Bold" said, "all."

Chapter Five

Breakfast was oatmeal, hot enough to peel the palate.

"We had eggs and bacon for a while," Bridger said, "but they finally ran out."

"The oatmeal should run out soon also, shouldn't it?" Pike asked.

"Undoubtedly," Bridger said, "but after that we'll just have to eat the same thing for breakfast that we eat for dinner—game!"

"Well," McConnell said, "at least it will be hot."

"That's one thing we won't ever run out of," Bridger said. "Hot. As long as we have water we'll have hot coffee, and as long as there is game we'll have hot meat."

Pike looked up and saw a few Crow braves watching them from a ridge. Yeah, he thought, and we'll have a hot time if the Crow Indians decide to come riding in.

He saw no reason to point out the scouts to Bridger and the rest. They knew they were out there just as well as he did.

It struck Pike that Bridger and his people had the same problem that the Indians had. They had no idea what kind of numbers the Crow had.

"Tell me something," he said to Bridger.

"What?"

"Have you sent out any scouts to see how many

Indians are in the Crow war party?"

"No," Bridger said, "I haven't seen the need. As long as we keep them in the dark as to our numbers, we needn't worry about theirs."

"Well, I suppose that's one way of looking at it," Pike said.

"You would send out scouts?"

Pike raised his hands and said, "Hey, I'm a guest here. You're booshway. You do what you feel is best for your people."

Bridger stared at Pike for a few moments and then said, "I'll give it some thought."

Pike grinned and said, "You've got oatmeal on your beard."

"So have you," Bridger said, "I just had too good manners to mention it to you."

It took five days for the camp to wear itself thin on Pike. If it hadn't been for the nights with Jeanna it wouldn't have taken that long.

He was tired of walking the camp in shifts. He would rather have taken his chances with just himself and McConnell.

He was tired of John Candy and all his questions. He wanted to leave and let Candy learn all he could from Bridger, who didn't seem to mind having the young pup on his tail.

He also didn't like staying in one place during the winter.

Then there was the matter of the tension.

There was a lot of it in camp, probably caused by the fact that they knew they were being watched by a Crow war party.

Up until now Jim Bridger had been able to keep the lid on well enough, but there were just too many people for that to last very long. In particular, there was a fellow named Sands who had four or five other men around him all the time, and they seemed particularly on edge. Sands was the big, burly type who liked to throw his weight around, looking as if he were in charge even when he wasn't — as was the case here. Bridger was in complete authority here, a position Pike did not envy. He liked being responsible for himself, and no one else. That was why he liked traveling with McConnell, who could take care of himself and make his own decisions — as evidenced by the bit with the blankets on the ice.

It all boiled down to Pike wanting to leave — with or without McConnell, who seemed to be enjoying the stay in camp — and Donna.

He woke that morning with Jeanna's warm body pressed tightly against his. He was enjoying that too much, which gave him another reason to leave, as well.

He moved a bit, knowing that she would wake immediately. He had learned that there was no way he could ever climb out of the blankets without waking her, so he stopped trying.

"Coffee?" she asked.

"Yes," he said.

She kissed his cheek and went out to get his coffee and his basin-or-bucket of water.

After he had drunk the coffee and cleaned up he said to her, "Jeanna, I have something to tell you."

"You're leaving?"

He looked at her in surprise and said, "Yes, how did you know?"

"I have seen it in you for days," she said, smiling. "I wonder that you have stayed here this long."

"I'm going to talk to Bridger this morning."

"And your friend?"

"I'll tell him I've decided to leave. He'll have to make his own decision."

"He will not abide by yours?"

"He's his own man, Jeanna," Pike said. "That's one

37

of the reasons I like traveling with him."

"He will go with you."

"What makes you say that?"

"I have been watching both of you," she said. "It may be true that he can make his own decisions, but it is clear to me that he belongs at your side."

"That's nonsense."

"We will see," she said. "Even Donna will not be able to keep him from leaving with you."

"We will see," he said.

Pike spoke to Bridger before McConnell.

"Well," Bridger said. "I'm disappointed, of course, but I understand. This is not our kind of gathering, Jack. Too many people."

"Too many restrictions," Pike said, then hurriedly added, "understandable restrictions, Jim, but too rigid for me."

"I know," Bridger said. "I'm asking for volunteers to do some scouting, as you suggested."

"I hope you get someone."

"Maybe you'd like to take that on before you leave?" Bridger asked. "You and Skins?"

"That's two things I'll have to ask Skins this morning," Pike said.

"He doesn't know that you decided to leave?"

"No."

"Why not?"

"We're not joined at the hip," Pike said. "We don't consult each other before making a decision. I've made mine, now it will be up to him to make his."

"He'll go with you," Bridger said.

"Are you so sure?" Pike asked. Bridger was the second person to tell him that with conviction.

"A choice between staying here with us or leaving with you?" Bridger said. "If I had that choice I'd certainly go with you."

Pike studied Bridger for a moment, wondering if the man was really sorry that he had chosen to winter here with so many people.

"I'll talk to Skins and get back to you about the scouting," Pike said.

"Don't feel any obligation to do it, Jack."

"That's easy enough," Pike said. "There is none."

Pike caught McConnell coming out of the tent he shared with Donna.

"How are your legs today?" Pike asked him the same question every morning.

"Pretty good," McConnell said. "I think I'm finally getting used to this."

"Before we go to breakfast," he said, "I want to tell you something."

"You've decided to leave," McConnell said.

Pike stared at his friend.

"Why is it everyone can read my mind this morning?" he asked with some annoyance.

"Because we've all seen how irritable and impatient you've been over the past few days," McConnell said. "I'm surprised you—"

"Don't say it," Pike said, holding his hand up. "I hate being predictable."

"You're not," McConnell said, and then added, "well, not always. When do you want to leave?"

"That depends," Pike said. "Are you coming?"

"Of course I'm coming," McConnell said. "You don't think I'd be able to stand it around here without you, do you?"

"Well," Pike said, "I *had* figured on leaving in the morning."

"What changed your mind?"

"Nothing, yet," Pike said. "Remember the suggestion I made to Bridger about sending out a scouting party of his own?"

"Sure," McConnell said. "Has he decided to go ahead and do it?"

"Yes."

McConnell started to look suspicious.

"Does he have someone in mind?" he asked, slowly.

"Yes, he does."

McConnell looked at Pike and said, "Not . . . us?"

"Yes, us," Pike said. "Of course, he doesn't want us to feel any obligation."

"What obligation?" McConnell asked. "There's no obligation for us to go out and take a chance of being captured by a Crow war party. Certainly not for five mornings of oatmeal."

"That's what I told him."

"And what did he say?"

"Nothing," Pike said. "I told him I'd talk to you about it and get back to him."

"Well, you know what to tell him."

"Sure I do," Pike said. "We'll do it . . . right?"

McConnell made a face and said, "Of course."

Chapter Six

"Supplies?" Bridger asked.

"Some dried meats," Pike said. "I don't intend for us to be out there very long."

"How will you find the Crow camp?" Candy asked.

"By looking," Pike said.

"Where?"

Bridger looked at Candy and said, "Why don't you go along and find out?"

"Now wait—" Pike started.

"I'd like to go," John Candy said, "very much."

"Now wait—" Pike said again.

"I don't think that's a very good idea," McConnell said.

"Why not?" Candy said.

"Because you're green," Pike said.

"You were green once," Bridger said.

Pike stared at Bridger across the fire. They were having dinner in front of his tent, the four of them, discussing what Pike and McConnell would need when they left the next morning. As far as Pike was concerned they would need as little as possible—and that meant *not* taking John Candy along.

"Let's take a walk," Bridger said to Pike.

As Candy started to rise McConnell put his hand on the man's arm.

"Just Bridger and Pike, son."

41

Pike rose and walked along with Bridger, away from the tent.

"Why do you want to saddle me with him?" Pike asked.

"I told you," Bridger said, "he's bright and he learns fast."

"He asks too many damned questions."

"How else is he gonna learn?" Bridger asked. "How else did you learn?"

"Don't compare him to me," Pike said.

"Why not?" Bridger said. "He reminds me of you and me when we were that age."

"We were never that young."

They walked for a few moments in silence.

"Look," Bridger said, "if he goes out there with you he'll come back worth more to me."

"If he comes back."

"It's only a scouting expedition, Jack," Bridger said. "You won't confront any of the Crow braves and, if you have your way, you won't be seen by any of them. Where's the harm in giving him a little education?"

They walked a bit longer. The moon was full and the ice of the Yellowstone seemed to glow.

"All right," Pike said, "I'll take him, but he's got to listen to every word I say."

"He will."

"I don't want him asking silly questions all the time."

"He won't," Bridger said. "I'll explain it all to him, Jack."

"All right," Pike said. "I want some coffee now."

"Let's go back."

Pike touched Bridger's arm and said, "If it comes down to a choice between him or McConnell, or him or me—"

Bridger said, "I understand that, Pike, but I don't anticipate any trouble, do you?"

"Always."

"I am glad we have one more night together under the blankets," Jeanna said.

"So am I," Pike said.

"I wish . . ." she began, and then stopped.

"What?" he asked. "What do you wish?"

"I wish that we could meet again in the spring, or the summer."

Pike squeezed her to him and said, "I'd like that myself, Jeanna."

She rolled atop him, mashing her breasts against his chest. She kissed him, his eyes, his nose, his chin, and then his mouth, hungrily, pushing her tongue deep into his mouth.

Between them he swelled and he reached down to take her by the hips and raise her up. When he let her down he slid into her easily, and he placed his hands on her smooth buttocks, rubbing them, kneading them as she rode him.

They began to sweat beneath the blankets, but neither of them cared. They continued to move against each other, urgently, demandingly, until finally she stiffened and bit him on the shoulder . . .

Later she touched the bite mark gently and said, "There, I have left my mark on you. You will carry it for a while."

"Proudly," he told her.

They went to sleep with her head on his chest and his arms around her.

In the morning he skipped his washing, but not the hot coffee. In fact, he had two cups, because he didn't know when he'd have another.

When he left the tent he saw John Candy with three horses saddled. Neither his nor the horse McConnell had ridden in on were among them.

"The three best animals in the string," Candy assured him.

"Fine," Pike said. "Go and fetch McConnell, will you?"

"Sure."

While Pike was checking the horses over, Bridger came along.

"Can't tell you how much I appreciate this, Jack," he said.

"And why not?" Pike said. "It was my damned idea, wasn't it?"

Bridger laughed.

"Candy pick these horses out himself?" Pike asked.

"He did," Bridger said. "He did a good job, eh?"

"So he knows horses," Pike said.

"Give him a chance, Jack," Bridger said. "He might surprise you."

"Jim Bridger," Pike said, "you know how I hate surprises."

Candy came along with McConnell at that moment.

"Are we ready?" McConnell asked.

"I guess so," Pike said.

They all mounted up and Pike looked down at Bridger.

"Tomorrow, the next day at the latest, depending on how far we have to go."

"We'll be on the lookout for you."

"Do that," Pike said, "because we could be coming in in a hurry."

Pike looked at John Candy, who could barely suppress the pleasure he was feeling.

He looked at McConnell and asked, "How are your legs, this morning?"

Part Two
Scouting Party

Chapter Seven

Iron Eagle watched as the three white men left the camp. In all the time that the Crow had been watching the white man's camp, this was the smallest party he had seen leave.

He turned and looked at the braves he had with him, six of the finest braves he had been able to pick. These men felt as he did, that their chief was being too cautious. They felt as Iron Eagle felt, that long ago they should have swooped in on the white man's camp and wiped it out.

Iron Eagle knew that these six braves would do whatever he asked of them. If he wanted them to kill the three white men, they would—and his first instinct was to do just that, but he knew what "The Bold" and the other, older braves would say. That he was headstrong, that he acted without thinking first.

Well, he would show them how wrong they were.

He motioned for his friend, Great Buffalo, to ride to his side.

"You see those three white men?" he asked, pointing.

"I see them, Iron Eagle," Great Buffalo said. "Say the word and we will kill them."

"No."

"No?" Great Buffalo said, puzzled. "But you have hungered for the white man's blood as much as we

45

have, Iron Eagle."

"And I still do," Iron Eagle said. "My blood runs as hot within me as does yours within you, my brother, but there is a way we may accomplish both our goals, and those of our chief."

"How?"

"By bringing those men back to our camp," Iron Eagle said. "They will tell our chief what he wants to know, and then we will be able to wipe out the white man's camp, as we have wanted . . . and Iron Eagle will show the elders that he can be as wise as they are."

"Then we will take them," Great Buffalo said.

"No," Iron Eagle said, "we will watch, and wait."

Puzzled even more Great Buffalo said, "I do not understand."

"Why would they send just three men out alone?" Iron Eagle said.

"To hunt."

"They have no provisions for hunting," Iron Eagle said. "They carry only their weapons, and blankets."

Great Buffalo pondered the question for some time, but shrugged his shoulders helplessly.

"They are a scouting party," Iron Eagle explained, patiently, "as are we. They have been sent out to find out our number."

"So?"

"So they will be looking for our camp."

"And?"

"And we will make sure that they are looking in the right direction."

Great Buffalo struggled mightily but in the end said, "I still do not understand."

"You do not have to, my brother," Iron Eagle said. "I will understand for you. You will simply do as I tell you to do."

Great Buffalo smiled, then. *That* he could understand.

"I will follow you loyally, as I have always done," he

46

said, proudly.

"Tell the others we will be moving soon," Iron Eagle said.

He would give the three men enough of a head start, and then begin to herd them toward their camp, as he would herd the buffalo . . . to their death.

Chapter Eight

"Where do we start looking?" John Candy asked.

They were only an hour out of camp and already he was starting to ask questions. Pike decided to give him the benefit of the doubt that this would not be the first of many, many questions, most of which would be silly.

"I figure we'll retrace our steps in the direction we came from after we encountered the Crow scouting party last week."

"Do you think they'll still be there?" Candy asked.

"No," Pike said, "but it's a direction to start in, and that's all we need right now, a starting point."

"I see."

"Or," McConnell said, "we could let the braves who are watching us now just herd us that way."

"Watched?" Candy asked, nervously. "We're being watched?"

He started to turn in his saddle and Pike snapped, "Don't turn around!"

Candy went stiff in his saddle.

"What are we going to do?" he asked.

"Well, for one thing," Pike said, "you're going to stop asking questions, right?"

"Uh, well, right."

"And you're going to listen to everything Skins and I tell you to do . . . right?"

"Right."

"Okay," Pike said, and they continued to ride along.

"Uh . . ." Candy said.

"What?" Pike asked.

"What is it you're going to tell me?"

"When I think of it," Pike said, "I'll let you know, all right?"

"Oh, uh, sure, all right," Candy said, "fine."

"They're still there, huh?" John Candy asked an hour later.

Pike knew the kid was just guessing, because he had no idea where the Indians were even if he did want to look at them.

"Candy . . ." Skins McConnell said, giving him a warning glance, and the younger man lapsed back into an uneasy, reluctant silence.

"They're keeping a respectful distance, Jack," McConnell said.

"That must be because we're heading in the right direction," Pike said. "Once we start going wrong I'm sure they'll do something to put us on the right track."

"Why?"

Pike and McConnell both looked at Candy.

"Well, I want to understand," the younger man said, defensively.

"All right," Pike said, "what's your question?"

"Why would they make sure that we were going in the right direction?" Candy asked. "Why would they want us to see their camp? And why don't they just kill us instead of following us?"

"Is that all you want to know?" Pike asked.

"For now."

Pike looked at McConnell, indicating that he wanted him to answer the questions.

"For one thing," McConnell said, "they're not concerned about us finding their camp, they want us *in* their camp, as prisoners."

"Oh, I see."

"And they're not killing us because they want to know how many men you have in your camp."

"So then, why are we—"

"Listen, Candy," Pike said, "we have a situation here that we're stuck with. We can't turn back because they wouldn't let us get through, anyway. We're just going to have to keep going and hope for the best."

Pike could tell by the look in Candy's eyes that he was spooked. He'd seen that look in the eyes of men and animals—such as horses—many, many times.

"Just take it easy," Pike said, his tone soothing, "try not to look nervous. Indians respect courage. Remember that."

"Yes, sir."

Pike hoped that Candy would keep quiet for a while. He knew that he and McConnell both needed some time to think this thing through.

They probably should have thought it through a little more before they agreed to take on this little scouting job. They could have simply left camp this morning and left all of this behind them.

Sure.

Pike knew that if they had left he would have worried about Jeanna and Bridger—and his people—until the next time he saw one of them. Also, even if they had left and ridden in the opposite direction, there was no guarantee that they wouldn't still have a small scouting party of Crow trailing them.

It was best not to berate himself for a bad decision. They would just have to continue on and make the best of a bad situation.

And that included having a green kid with them.

Skins McConnell hadn't counted on having to play middle man to Pike and John Candy. He knew that

Pike had only agreed to take Candy along as a favor to Bridger, but McConnell had been sure it was a bad idea, and he was being proved correct.

McConnell dropped back to ride behind the kid as Pike took the lead. Candy was as skittish as a newborn calf, and in the event that he broke and tried to run, they were going to have to stop him.

If the Crow saw any sign of fear, they would be all over them before they knew what was happening. In a situation like that it was very likely that somebody would end up dead.

Candy felt panicky.

Beneath the layers of clothing he was sweating. He could smell it and he knew it was fear, he just hoped that Pike and McConnell couldn't smell it, as well.

He wondered if Indians could smell fear.

He wanted to do two things. He wanted to turn around and try to see where the Indians were, and then he wanted to run. He didn't even want to wait for his horse, he just wanted to jump down from the saddle and start running.

He got hold of himself and kept his eyes straight. They were riding single file at this point, and he was riding between Pike, who was in the lead, and McConnell, who was bringing up the rear. He thought that they had probably maneuvered him into that position to keep him from bolting. Even if they couldn't smell his fear the way he himself could, they surely knew that he was frightened. Why else would he have continued to ask so many questions, even after promising himself that he would not?

He took a deep breath and tried to relax. Even if the Indians came after them, Pike and McConnell had assured him that death was not imminent. They would first be taken to the Crow camp, where the Indians would question them as to the manpower in the camp.

As long as they were alive, and in control of themselves, there was a chance that they would be able to escape from this predicament.

John Candy tried to take comfort from the fact that he was out here with Jack Pike, who was every bit the legend in these mountains that Jim Bridger was.

It helped.

A little.

Pike stopped and both Candy and McConnell continued on until they were flanking him.

"Skins, have you gotten a count?"

"Six, maybe seven," McConnell replied.

"That's what I figure," Pike said. "Not as bad as it might be."

"Don't we have an advantage in knowing that they're there?" Candy asked.

"What kind of advantage is that, kid?" Pike asked.

"Well . . . they don't know that we know that they're there, do they?"

Pike and McConnell exchanged a glance and Pike said, "If I understand you correctly, of course they know we know they're there."

"But if they know that we know, why don't they just come down and get us?"

"Because we must still be going in the right direction," Pike said. He turned away from Candy to look at McConnell. "I think we should cross the river. The chances are good that they're camping on the other side."

"Agreed."

Pike turned away from McConnell to look at Candy and said, "Okay?"

Candy, surprised at being consulted, said, "Uh, yeah, sure."

Chapter Nine

"They know we are watching," Great Buffalo said.

"Of course they know," Iron Eagle said. "The bigger man in front, look at the way he sits his horse. See how he never looks behind him, and yet he knows that we are here."

"We should take them, then," Great Buffalo said.

"No," Iron Eagle said, "they are crossing the ice, still moving in the right direction. We will continue to follow, and watch." He looked at the other man and said, "Tell the others. I want no mistakes. No one is to do anything unless I give the word."

"Yes, my brother."

Great Buffalo went to relay the instructions to the other braves, all of whom were impatient for some kind of action.

Iron Eagle watched the three white men cross the ice, noticing how the big man in front went first, allowing the other two to follow only after he had made it all the way across without incident.

Iron Eagle felt a kinship with the big white man. He cared for his men the way Iron Eagle himself did. He was also a big man, as the Crow brave was, and Iron Eagle found himself looking forward to talking with the man, and questioning him.

How long would the man last, he wondered, before he told them what they wanted to know?

Chapter Ten

As darkness started to fall Pike and McConnell wondered if they would be allowed to camp for the night in peace.

They had travelled so much and so often together that it was almost as if they could read each other's minds.

"The only way we're gonna find out if they'll let us camp is to try it," McConnell said.

"Then let's try it," Pike said.

"If we camp, won't they be able to sneak up on us in the dark?" Candy asked.

"If they wanted us they would have made a try by now," Pike said, patiently.

"Also," McConnell said, "if we keep traveling in the dark one of our animals is bound to break a leg."

"Let's find a place," Pike said.

It took another hour before they found a likely place to camp. There was a small depression in the ground against a rock face. Both the depression and the face would give them some shelter from the wind.

"Candy, take care of the horses," Pike said. "McConnell and I will get some wood for a fire."

"Right."

It didn't really take the two of them to collect wood for the fire, but Pike wanted to take advantage of the darkness to try and get a closer look at the Indians who were following them.

Actually, they weren't really being followed so much as they were being herded. Pike was almost tempted to change direction and see what the Indians would do. Maybe it would have been better to confront them. Three against six or seven was certainly not odds that were in their favor, but neither were they insurmountable.

Still, the sound of gunfire would more than likely be heard by the main body of Crow braves in their camp. Although they had put some distance between themselves and Bridger's camp, the white men might even hear the shots. The last thing Pike wanted was to have both camps come running. All that would produce would be a lot of dead men on both sides.

Pike began to walk back the way they had come, picking up some pieces of dead wood here and there, trying to look like he was just collecting wood for a fire. Meanwhile, he was looking to see where the braves had chosen to stop and watch them from. There was a ridge above them that would make a fine vantage point, but it wouldn't be a good place to camp. Pike assumed that one brave would be left on the ridge to watch while the others camped some distance away. He continued to watch from the corner of his eye until he finally caught some movement and then, satisfied that he was correct in his assumption, he returned to camp with his small bundle of wood.

He dropped his small load onto McConnell's larger one and crouched down to start the fire.

"There's at least one brave on that ridge above us," he told McConnell.

"Got a guess as to where the others are?"

"Probably found someplace to camp nearby," Pike said, "far enough away so that we won't hear them or smell them, but close enough so that if we start to move they'll know about it quick enough."

"Smell them?" Candy asked. He had walked up on

58

them at the tail end of the statement.

Pike looked up and said, "In case they make a fire, they wouldn't want us to smell it."

"Oh," Candy said. "Well, what about our fire? What if they smell it?".

Pike looked at McConnell, who said to Candy, "John, they already know where we are."

"Oh," Candy said, "that's right."

"Can you get a fire going?" Pike asked him.

"Of course."

"Then do it," Pike said, and backed away from the job. McConnell followed him.

"What do you want to do?" McConnell asked.

Pike spread his blanket on the ground and said, "Well, we could wait until the middle of the night and walk the horses for a while. We might be able to get away without being seen."

"That Crow brave on the ridge isn't gonna fall asleep," McConnell said.

"No," Pike said, "I don't believe so."

McConnell spread his blanket and sat down next to Pike, leaning back against his saddle.

"What if," he said, slowly, "one of us got up on that ridge and put him to sleep?"

Pike looked at McConnell and a smile slowly spread over his face, splitting his beard.

"I could probably work my way behind him—"

"Why you?" McConnell asked. "It was my idea."

"I can move more quietly than you can."

"Who says?" McConnell added. "You outweigh me by forty pounds."

At that point John Candy came over. They looked beyond him and saw the fire burning.

"I couldn't help overhearing," the younger man said. "I can move real quiet."

"Forget it," Pike said. "This is between McConnell and me. You'll stay in camp."

"But—"

"You're supposed to be doing what you're told, kid!" Pike said. "Tend the fire."

Candy turned and trudged dejectedly to the fire.

"A little rough on him, weren't you?" McConnell asked.

"What should I do? Let him go up there and get killed? Maybe get us killed?"

"No."

"Then don't be telling me how rough I am," Pike said. "Let's get this settled. One of us is going up there after that Crow brave. Which one?"

"Let's settle it the fair way," McConnell said.

He walked over to where they had piled the wood for the fire and began pulling smaller pieces off it. When he came back he showed Pike six twigs. Five were roughly the same length while the sixth was noticeably shorter.

"Give me your hat," McConnell said.

Pike hesitated a moment, then took off his hat. The cold hair on his bare head was shocking.

McConnell dropped the six twigs into the hat and then extended it to Pike. They would continue to draw sticks until someone got the short one. That would be the man who went after the brave.

On the third pick, the short stick showed up.

Chapter Eleven

Dancing Horse did not relish the task that he had been given. Even wrapped in his blanket, the cold bit into his flesh as he watched the three white men from his perch on the ridge. He thought of his brothers, sitting near a warm fire, while he froze up here. Still, he could not have refused when Iron Eagle chose him for the task. If the weather had been even a little less cold he would have counted the selection as an honor.

He looked down longingly at the white man's fire and wondered why they were not sitting closer to it, as he would have been.

He continued to watch them, secure in the knowledge that he would not be chosen for the next such task, having already been given this one.

At least he hoped not.

They waited until about two a.m. and then McConnell rose and went to the fire to pour himself a cup of coffee. Pike watched his friend from his blanket, wishing it had been he who had drawn the short stick.

Candy was on watch at that point, and he simply watched as McConnell drank the coffee.

"I'm going to check the horses," McConnell said to Candy.

Now they knew that the Indian on the ridge would

not be able to hear the words that were being spoken, but they hoped that he would understand the body language.

The horses had been picketed against the rock wall in the hopes of protecting them as well as themselves from the wind. McConnell moved in among the three animals, and at that moment felt he was effectively shielded from the prying eyes of the Crow brave.

He ducked low and moved behind the animals, and away from the camp. He had his Kentucky pistol in his belt, but he hoped to be able to avoid using that. Instead, he had his knife along as well, as he wanted to use that in dispatching the Crow brave.

There was no question in McConnell's mind but that he was going to kill the brave. He wanted to take no chance that the man could sound any kind of an alarm.

The other reason they had waited until two a.m. was that it would give the Indians time to bring on a relief, if that was going to be the case. They had no way of knowing whether or not the same brave would be up there all night.

Dancing Horse watched as the white men exchanged places at one point during the night. Apparently, the whites took turns with the watch, and while the Crow disdained such actions, Dancing Horse found that — on this night — he would not have minded it so much. Of course, he would not ask to be relieved. That would certainly be a show of weakness on his part. If, however, relief had been offered him, he would have gladly taken it.

He knew, though, that would never happen.

McConnell started his climb, which would be a fairly simple one. There were enough foot- and handholds along the way to assure that he would make the ascent in decent time. The problem they had to face was if the brave started to wonder why he was in among the horses for so long.

They had discussed that possibility . . .

"You'll have to get to him before he gets suspicious," Pike had said.

"I know."

"I'll try to keep an eye on him," Pike said. "If he looks as if he's going to raise the alarm, I'll have to pin him down with rifle fire. Leave me your rifle, and I'll have Candy reload while I fire."

"I can fire a rifle," Candy said, in annoyance.

"That's not at question here, John," Pike said, "but it would serve no purpose for both of us to fire when only one shot is needed to pin him down. If you continue to reload, I can keep him up there until McConnell gets back."

"And then what?" Candy said. "They'll know what we tried to do."

"That's right," Pike said, "and at that point it will be up to them to call the action. We won't have any control over the situation at all."

Climbing to the ridge, McConnell wondered if they had any control over the situation even now. Pike said there was only one brave on watch, and he was usually right about those things, but for all McConnell really knew there was *more* than one brave waiting for him up there. If he got there and found himself faced with three or four of them he was going to be shit out of luck.

If they tossed him off the ridge, he was going to try and land right on Pike's head.

Dancing Horse pulled his blanket closer around him and sneaked a glance at the sky. He had been hoping that he would see daylight somewhere up there, but it was not to be. There were hours to go before daylight.

Dancing Horse looked back down at the white man's camp and he suddenly wondered where the third man was. He had apparently gone to check on the horses, but that had been a long time ago.

He shucked off the blanket and got up onto his knees to try and get a better look. He saw one man on watch and one man underneath his blankets. He could see the third man's blanket, but it didn't look as if the man was beneath it.

Where had he gone?

Dancing Horse reached next to him for his rifle but as he did he felt someone's hand close over his wrist.

"Wha—" he said, turning his head.

McConnell pulled on the man's arm, jerking him toward him, and buried his knife deep into his belly. The Indian opened his mouth as if to yell and Mc-Connell brought the knife up, slicing the man open and turning his cry into a strangled whisper. As the man's weight fell against him he lowered him to the ground and pulled his knife free, then kicked the rifle over the edge.

Pike heard something strike the ground and looked up quickly. He was relieved to see McConnell stand up and wave to him.

Pike came out of his blanket quickly and said to Candy. "He got him. Douse the fire. We're going to move out."

"In the dark?" Candy asked. "But I thought you said it was too dangerous—"

"It's too dangerous to ride," Pike said. "We're going

64

to walk the horses until first light."

"But—"

"Just get that fire out and collect your gear."

Pike rolled up his blanket and McConnell's. By the time McConnell climbed back down he had both of their horses saddled.

"What?" Pike said.

"He's dead," McConnell said.

"What fell?"

"I kicked his rifle over the edge. One less rifle, right?"

"Right."

"They have rifles?" Candy asked. "I thought they'd have bows and arrows."

"They do," Pike said patiently, "but they have rifles, too."

"Where do they get rifles?"

Pike looked at McConnell, who shrugged.

"Tell him where they get rifles from, Skins."

"From white men," McConnell said.

"What?" Candy said, looking aghast. "White men give them rifles?"

"Sell, Candy," McConnell said, "they sell them the rifles."

Pike stared at Candy, wondering if he was really as naive as he sounded. Was anyone ever as naive as John Candy sounded?

"Walk easy, John," Pike said. He spoke slowly, as if he were speaking to a child. "You'll be walking behind me. Don't rush. If your horse stops, don't pull him, stop with him. If he stops he's stopping for a reason."

"Right."

"If I stop I'll call out, so you don't walk up my back."

"Okay."

"I'll be behind you," McConnell said. "If you're going to stop, sing out. If I stop, I'll let you know and you let Pike know."

"All right."

"Do you understand all of this?" Pike asked.

"Of course I do," Candy said. "I'm not stupid, you know."

No, Pike thought, just naive!

The walk through the dark was hazardous, but with Pike in the lead—and with Candy doing everything he was told to do—they managed to avoid injuries to them and their animals.

When the sun finally put in an appearance Pike called a halt to their procession.

"Time to mount up."

"Do you think we lost them?" Candy asked.

"I hope so," Pike said, even though he doubted it. The best they could hope for was to find the Crow camp, assess the situation and get back to their own camp before the Crow braves caught up to them. They were going to be real angry when they discovered the body of their brother.

They mounted up.

"We'll stay single file," Pike said.

"Where are we going to look now?" Candy asked. "We don't have them to herd us in the right direction."

"We'll look around for the rest of today, Candy, and then we go back."

"Without finding out what we came to find out?"

"That's right," Pike said. "I've got a life to get on with. I'm doing this as a favor to Bridger."

"Well," Candy said, "when we get back I'll take a couple of men out and try again. After all, I've been through it once, I know how to go about it."

Pike opened his mouth to reply, but then thought better of it. If this kid was cocky enough to think he'd actually learned something, let him go out and get killed.

Then he'd really learn something.

Chapter Twelve

They stopped for a lunch of dried meat and water and didn't bother to unsaddle the horses.

"We'll just give them a little blow and then be on our way again," Pike said. He took a couple of pieces of meat and said, "I'm going to walk back and check our back trail."

McConnell and Candy both watched until Pike was out of sight.

"Skins, tell me something," Candy said.

"What?"

"What's he got against me?"

"You really wanna know?"

"Yeah. I mean, I haven't done anything to him that I know of—have I?"

"Maybe not," McConnell said. "he just didn't want you along, is all."

"Why not?"

"Because he doesn't want to have to take the time to answer your questions, to educate you."

"How else am I going to learn?"

McConnell smiled and said, "From someone else, Candy, not from him. He considers keeping himself alive a major responsibility. He doesn't need any others."

"What about you?"

"What about me?"

"He lets you ride with him."

"Why shouldn't he?"

"You just said he doesn't want the responsibility of keeping anyone else alive."

"He doesn't have the responsibility with me," McConnell said. "I keep myself alive, kid. Sometimes I even keep him alive. Why, he's even been known to save my life a time or two, but generally speaking we look out for ourselves."

"I didn't mean to offend you."

"You didn't," McConnell said, "not really, no more than you offend him. You bother us, Candy. You ask questions, you get answers, but we're not convinced that you really hear what we're saying."

"Bridger says I'm a good listener."

"I know," McConnell said, "he told us that, too. He's convinced . . . we're not."

"So what do I do to prove myself?"

"I don't think you can, kid," McConnell said. "Not to me and not to him, not this trip. You just don't have enough time."

Pike appeared once again and rejoined them. He gave them each a look, and decided not to ask what they were talking about.

"Nothing?" McConnell asked.

"Not a sign."

"That's good, isn't it?"

Pike frowned, then looked at McConnell.

"I didn't really expect to shake them, Skins."

"I know."

"Then why did we—"

"We went through the motions, kid," McConnell said. "It's what you're supposed to do."

"So what now?"

Pike ignored Candy.

"What do you think, Jack?" McConnell said.

Pike rubbed his jaw and said, "I think the sons of bitches are ahead of us."

"Ahead of us?" Candy said.

"I think they left one man behind to watch us, and kept moving."

Candy stared wild-eyed ahead of them, and neither Pike nor McConnell told him not to. It wouldn't have done any good.

"If they're ahead of us they're good, because I haven't seen any sign of them," McConnell said.

"Well, Skins," Pike said, "they are Crow Indians and we're just a couple of white men — but they're there. I'm convinced."

"So what's our next move?" McConnell asked.

"You tell me."

"Well," McConnell said, "if they're up ahead, I say we go back the way we came."

Pike finally looked at Candy.

"What do you say, Junior?"

Candy squared his jaw and said, "I say we keep going."

"Why?"

Defiantly Candy said, "Because you can't be right all the time. You say they're ahead of us. What if they're still behind us? What if we turn around and go back and ride right into them?"

Pike looked at McConnell, who said, "Hey, don't look at me. The kid's got a point . . . sort of."

"Do you still vote to go back?"

"Sure."

"All right," Pike said. "One vote to go back and one to go ahead. I'm the tie-breaker, and I say we go back. We're calling this off. It was a bad idea to begin with."

McConnell shrugged and said, "That's what you get for doing favors."

"Let's get the hell out of here," Pike said.

He and McConnell started to mount up when John Candy said, "No!"

"What?" Pike said, staring at him.

Candy stood his ground and said, "I'm not turning

back. I came out here to find something out, and I'm going ahead, with or without you."

Pike moved close to Candy, so close that their noses almost touched.

"You're going back, Candy, *with* us, because you aren't going *anywhere* without us. Do you understand?"

"It's you who doesn't understand, Pike," Candy said. "I'm going on."

Pike glared at Candy until the younger man averted his eyes reluctantly.

"Where are you from?" Pike asked.

"What?" Candy looked puzzled by the question.

"Where are you from . . . I mean, originally?"

"Uh—why—St. Louis."

"And you came out here because you want to be a mountain man, huh?" Pike asked.

"I like the mountains," Candy said. "I wanted to learn to live in them. What's wrong with that?"

"If you go on while we go back—and we are going back, Candy, believe me—then all you're going to learn is how to die in the mountains."

Pike paused to let that sink in. Candy was not looking at Pike, but his jaw had the set and his shoulders the slump of a child who has been called on the carpet—a child who knows he's wrong but won't admit it.

"Now, get your ass on your horse, sonny, we're heading back—now!"

Candy looked at Pike then and Pike knew he was going to have to knock the stubbornness out of him. It was the only way to keep him alive.

"I'm not—"

Pike didn't let him finish. He backhanded the younger man across the face, knocking Candy to the ground. Blood leaked from his cut lip and his eyes were glazed.

"Let's get him up and onto his horse," Pike said.

"I don't think so, Jack."

Pike looked at McConnell and frowned.

"Why not, Skins?"

McConnell wasn't looking at Pike, but beyond him. Wordlessly, he jerked his chin and Pike looked behind him at six Crow braves. They had come from the direction in which they were going and not from where they had come.

"Well," Pike said, "I was right about one thing."

"What?" McConnell asked, keeping his eyes on the Indians.

"They were ahead of us."

McConnell looked at Pike then and said, "And they still are."

Chapter Thirteen

None of the braves said a word. They must have been watching for some time. They all held rifles in the crooks of their arms. One brave stood a little ahead of the others, a man almost as big as Pike himself. His eyes were on Pike.

They had two choices. They could go for their rifles and die trying, or they could simply give up and hold onto life a little bit longer. As long as there was life, there was a chance.

Pike looked at McConnell and the two of them moved away from where their rifles were, propped against a large stone. Pike reached a hand down to Candy.

"Get up, kid," he said. "You win. We're going ahead."

Candy got to his feet and wiped the blood from his mouth. He looked at the six braves, and then at Pike and McConnell and said, "If you call this winning, I don't want to be around when you lose."

They were allowed to ride to the Crow camp, and as they entered they became the center of attention. Men and women stared at them and children ran up to them and along with them, staring and chattering.

None of the braves who had captured them had yet

said a word to them. Their guns and weapons had been collected and then the big buck had waved them to mount up.

Now the big buck dismounted and waved at them to do the same.

"Do either of you speak Crow?" Candy asked as they dismounted.

Still asking questions, Pike thought wearily.

"Some," he said.

"So why don't we try to talk to them?"

"Because they are obviously not ready to talk to us yet," Pike said.

"They're in control, John," McConnell said. "Now shut up and wait."

They were pushed toward a lodge and then one brave moved to the entrance and waved them in. When they stepped inside they found it empty, bare and quite cold.

"How are we supposed to—" Candy began to ask, turning, but no one was listening to him—not the Crow, not McConnell and certainly not Pike.

"Better find a warm corner," Pike said to both of them. "I think we're going to be here a while."

McConnell picked a spot and sat on the ground, followed by Pike. Candy remained standing, still wanting to understand the situation.

"Are they just going to leave us in here?"

"For a while," McConnell said.

"We'll freeze."

"Two of us might," McConnell said, "but they'll make sure one of us stays alive to be questioned."

"But we have to—"

"Sit down, kid," Pike said.

Candy stared at him.

"Come on, sit down," Pike said. "Let's talk."

"Now you want to talk?" Candy asked, incredulously.

"Well," Pike said, "we have nothing else to do."

"Besides," McConnell said, "we can use all the hot air we can generate in here, can't we?"

Candy stared at both of them as if they were crazy, and then finally sat down.

They talked for about three hours.

John Candy got more than he bargained for, lessons in everything from hunting and fishing to surviving on next to nothing in the mountains.

After a few moments of silence had passed Pike looked at Candy and said, "What, no more questions?"

Candy shook his head.

"I'm all questioned out," he said. "I can't even think any more, I'm so cold."

"Let's be grateful that they decided to let us wait inside," McConnell said.

Candy thought about that for a moment and then shuddered, hugging himself.

"Hey, kid," Pike said.

"What?"

"I'm sorry I hit you."

"Forget it," Candy said. "You were right, they were ahead of us. If I had gone on I'd probably be dead."

"There's a good chance you would have, yeah," McConnell said, "but that doesn't matter, anymore."

"What are they gonna do?" Candy asked.

Pike looked at McConnell and said, "I knew he'd come up with another question."

"I just—"

"Relax, kid," Pike said, "I'll answer it. They're going to let us stew a while, and then they'll offer us hot food, blankets, maybe even some warm, willing squaws."

"For what?"

"For the information they want," Pike said. "How many men Bridger has."

"We can't tell them!"

"I know we can't tell them," Pike said, "and I hope

you'll understand that there's no offense intended, but I know that Skins and I won't tell them anything—how about you?"

"I'll never tell them anything!" Candy said, indignantly.

"Well, you see, after being nice doesn't work they'll try something else," McConnell said.

"Like what?"

"Like pain," Pike said. "What's your threshold for pain, Candy?"

The younger man stared at both of them wide-eyed.

"I—I, uh, don't know."

"Well, you may find out soon enough," Pike said.

"W-what do I do?"

"You do what we're going to do," Pike said. "When they get to the pain part you put up with as much of it as you can."

"And then?"

"And then," McConnell said, "you lie."

"Lie?"

"Uh, you have lied before, haven't you?" McConnell asked.

Candy looked blank.

"To your parents?" McConnell said. "A woman, maybe? A teacher?"

"I don't think I've ever . . . had a reason to lie before."

"Well, try coming out of this alive," Pike said. "How's that for a reason?"

"Well . . . I'll try."

"Don't try," McConnell said. "If you're going to lie to these Indians, you've got to make them believe you."

"How do I do that?"

"When they start to hurt you, don't give in too easily," Pike said. "If you start talking too soon they'll know you're lying."

"H-how long do I wait?"

"That's going to be up to you to decide, John," Pike

said. "Take as much as you can and then lie your damned head off."

"All right," Candy said, "but there's one other thing."

"What's that?" Pike asked.

"What do I say?" Candy asked. "I mean, when I lie. What do I say?"

They spent the next two hours trying to teach John Candy how to lie, and then what to lie about.

"Let's make a bet," Pike said.

He could hardly feel his fingertips.

"A bet?" Candy asked. "What kind of bet?"

He wiggled his toes inside his boots—at least, he thought he was wiggling his toes.

"I think I know," McConnell said.

He touched his nose, happy to find that it was still there. He'd been afraid it might have frozen solid and fallen off.

"Which one of us they'll come for first?" McConnell asked.

"That's what I had in mind."

"You mean," Candy said, "they won't question us together?"

Pike and McConnell exchanged long-suffering glances.

"John," Pike said, "what good is lying going to do us if we all tell different lies?"

"They'd know right away we were lying."

"Right," McConnell said. "See, what we told you to say is what we're going to say, as well."

Candy looked at both of them and said, "Well, that should work."

Chapter Fourteen

They were in the lodge six hours before someone appeared. When one of the braves did show up it was the big buck who had obviously been the leader of the scouting party. He entered, straightened up and stared down at the three seated, nearly frozen men.

"I am Iron Eagle."

"Congratulations," Pike said.

The brave frowned, apparently not understanding the word.

"I have hot food for you," he said, "and blankets."

"And what do we have to do for them?" Pike asked.

"You must answer one question."

"And what would that be?" McConnell asked.

"What is the strength of your camp?"

The brave looked at each of them in turn, waiting for an answer. When none was forthcoming he tossed back the flap of the lodge and waved someone in.

She was a pretty squaw, with dark skin and hair like Jeanna. In her hands she was holding several wooden bowls from which steam was rising. Obviously, the bowls held hot food. The aroma of whatever it was insinuated itself into each of their noses, but even more, they could feel the heat emanating from the food.

Pike looked quickly at Candy, who was staring at the woman holding the bowls.

"Actually," Pike said to Iron Eagle, "we're not all that hungry."

Iron Eagle waved someone else in. This time a less pretty squaw entered with blankets.

"Forget it, Iron Eagle," Pike said, deciding to do away with the jokes. "We're not interested in your food, or your blankets."

Iron Eagle stared at Pike, and Pike held his eyes, answering the challenge he saw there.

"Very well," the Crow brave said. He said something to each of the squaws. The one with the bowls of food put one down on the ground, and the one with the blanket put one down, also. They withdrew then, and Iron Eagle followed them.

Candy leaped forward and Pike and McConnell both stopped him.

"Easy, kid," Pike said. "They want us to fight over it, but we're going to share it."

"Sure, sure," Candy said, "I was going to share."

"Skins," Pike said, "you do the honors."

McConnell picked up the bowl of meat and separated it into three equal parts. Pike took his and then Candy hastily took his. McConnell picked up his and they all wolfed the meager fare down. At least it was hot, even if it was somewhat gamey.

"We'll have to sit close together to share the one blanket," McConnell said.

"Let the kid sit in the middle," Pike said.

"Why?" Candy asked.

Pike stared at him and said, "Because I thought if I said that you were sitting on the end then you'd ask why. In the middle you'll get the benefit of our body warmth as well as the blanket."

"But why should—"

"Jesus, don't argue with me, kid, all right?" Pike said.

Candy didn't argue and they sat down and spread the blanket over the three of them. McConnell and

80

Pike still had one arm exposed, but it was better than nothing.

"W-why did they give us the food and blanket?" Candy asked.

"They don't want us to be comfortable, John," Pike said, "but they do want to keep us alive—that is, until they decide which one of us they have the better chance of cracking."

Candy looked at Pike and McConnell and said, "And you figure that'll be me, right?"

"Pike and I have been through this, kid," McConnell said, "have you?"

"No," Candy mumbled, "no, I haven't."

"Then who would you say is the weak link here?"

"Me," Candy said, and then added, "theoretically."

"What does that mean?" McConnell asked. "Theoretically?"

"Well," Candy said, "the way I see it, there's less chance of my breaking than there is of either of you."

"How do you figure that?" Pike asked, with interest.

"See, if you break you've got no one to answer to," Candy said.

"And you do?"

"If I break," Candy said, "I'll never hear the end of it from you guys."

"What did they tell you?" "The Bold" asked.

"They told me nothing," Iron Eagle said. "I did not expect them to tell me anything."

"Why not?"

"Their leader, he is a strong man. They will follow him."

"You can tell this, already?"

"I can tell this by looking at him," Iron Eagle said, with certainty.

"Good," "The Bold" said, "then they shall follow him to their deaths."

81

Part Three
Crow Captives

Chapter Fifteen

When Iron Eagle came back two hours later he brought two other braves with him. They entered and stared down at the three mountain men, who were huddled beneath the one blanket.

Pike and McConnell stared back, while Candy's eyes wandered a bit. In spite of the brave front he was trying to put up, he wasn't all that sure that he'd be able to perform the way Pike and McConnell had explained. John Candy had never in his life experienced real pain. He didn't know what would happen when the time came.

He hoped they wouldn't take him first.

Iron Eagle pointed to McConnell and the two braves moved forward and hauled McConnell to his feet.

"See you soon, partner," McConnell said to Pike.

"Spit in his eye for me," Pike said.

After they were gone Candy said, "What if he doesn't come back?"

"For Chrissake, kid, when are you going to stop asking dumb questions?" Pike said.

An hour later the flap of the lodge was thrown back and McConnell came stumbling through. He went sprawling on the ground and Pike could see that a couple of his fingers were bloody and bent at a wrong angle. On top of that there was blood on his face and on his shirt.

"Jesus," Candy said beneath his breath.

Iron Eagle stepped in with the same two braves and pointed to Pike.

"Nothin'," McConnell mumbled, "didn't tell them nothin', Jack!"

"I hear you, Skins," Pike said as the two braves pulled him to his feet.

As they were pushing him out of the lodge Pike said to Candy over his shoulder, "Do what you can for him, kid. I'll see you in a while."

When they were gone John Candy looked down at McConnell, who was suddenly very still.

He wondered if he was dead.

Suddenly, he felt very alone.

Pike was half dragged and half walked through camp to another, bigger lodge, and pushed through the entrance. Inside one man was waiting for him. He turned and saw that neither Iron Eagle nor the other two braves had entered after him.

He looked at the Indian he was with and saw that he was about twenty years older than the bunch who had brought them in.

"I am called 'The Bold'," the man said. "I am chief here."

Pike bit back a smart response. This was neither the time nor the place to antagonize the man.

"Sit."

Pike sat, confused. McConnell had obviously been worked out pretty thoroughly. Now a new tack was being taken with him.

"You are the leader?"

The question sounded rhetorical, so even though it wasn't strictly true Pike said, "Yes." If they were

84

going to key their efforts on one man, it would be the leader. This way maybe he was taking a little pressure off McConnell and Candy.

"Iron Eagle thinks you are a great leader," "The Bold" said.

"I am flattered," Pike said, "but I am not so sure he is right."

"Why do you say this?"

Pike spread his arms and said, "Look where I have led them."

"You would have to be a great leader and a great warrior to outsmart Iron Eagle," "The Bold" said. "He is young, and strong, and sometimes foolhardy, but he is also very smart."

"You speak English very well," Pike said. "You and Iron Eagle both."

"We learned from you, or from men like you," "The Bold" said. "If you are to defeat your enemy you must be able to think like him, move like him, even speak like him. That is true whether your enemy is a man or an animal."

"You are not my enemy."

"You," "The Bold" said, "are mine."

"Are we talking about me personally, or my people?"

"The white man and red man will always be enemies. It is the way."

"There have been treaties."

"They have all been broken," "The Bold" said. "There is only one way that there can be peace between us."

"What is that?"

"If only one of us survives."

"That is unfortunate," Pike said.

"Yes," "The Bold" said, "for you."

Pike shuddered.

"I must ask you what the strength of your camp is," the chief said.

"I cannot answer that."

"I know," "The Bold" said, "but I must ask, and continue to ask. If you do not tell me, I will have to let Iron Eagle ask you."

"As he asked my friend?"

"Yes."

"Then let him ask," Pike said. "I will give him the same answers my friend did."

"Your friend told Iron Eagle everything we wanted to know."

"No," Pike said, smiling grimly and shaking his head, "he did not."

They locked eyes for a moment, and neither man backed down. Pike didn't know what other men saw when they looked into his eyes, but he looked into the eyes of the man called "The Bold" and saw cold, and he saw death.

"Leave my lodge," the chief finally said. "Iron Eagle is waiting for you outside."

Pike stood up. As he moved to the lodge entrance he glanced back at "The Bold", but the man was not watching him. He was staring off into space, looking at something only he could see.

Pike wondered whose future he was looking at.

Chapter Sixteen

Outside Iron Eagle was waiting, with his two warriors. "Where to now?" Pike asked.

"Now," Iron Eagle said, "we go to *my* lodge."

Pike's arms were gripped on both sides and he was again propelled across the camp. He wasn't sure how many hours they had been there, but it was dark and the camp looked deserted. Everyone must have been inside their lodges, keeping warm.

When they reached Iron Eagle's lodge he was pushed inside. This time Iron Eagle and the other two men followed him in. There was a fire going and Iron Eagle stepped around to the other side of it. Pike was left standing, with a brave on each side of him.

Iron Eagle was almost his size, and the two braves were not much smaller. He had the feeling they had been chosen specifically for their size. He doubted that he'd be able to take all three of them in that confined space.

He stood still and waited.

"I must ask you again—"

"I know the question, Iron Eagle," Pike said. "I heard it from you, and I heard it from your chief. Is he really called 'The Bold'?"

"He is."

"What's his real name?"

"That is the name he is known by."

"Did you pick it himself?"

Iron Eagle did not answer. Instead he said something to

87

the other two men. By the time Pike — with his limited knowledge of the Crow language — figured it out, they had him by the arms, stretching them about as far as they would go. They were each holding him by the wrist, which was bent back, and by the fingers.

Pike thought he knew what had happened to McConnell's hand.

"One word from me," Iron Eagle said, "and they will break your fingers, one by one."

"It must be nice to have that kind of power," Pike said.

"I will use that power in moderation," Iron Eagle said. "I will ask you a question. If you do not answer it I will have one finger broken. I will ask again. If again you do not answer, I will have another broken. I do not know if you noticed, but your friend had two broken fingers."

"If that's supposed to make me believe that he talked after only two fingers, I'll have to call you a liar, Iron Eagle."

The man moved like a cat, fast for his or *any* size. He leaped over the fire and buried his fist into Pike's belly. Pike tried to double over, but the men holding his arms would not allow it.

"You would be wise not to call me a liar again," Iron Eagle said, putting his mouth right next to Pike's right ear.

Pike tried to speak, but didn't have enough air yet. He breathed in and out carefully, until he thought he could speak, and then tried again.

"Then I'd have to say I don't believe you."

"Why not?"

"Because I know my friend."

"Do you?"

"Very well," Pike said. "He wouldn't have talked — not after only two fingers. In fact, I don't think he would have talked after ten fingers."

"Then perhaps I should have two of yours broken right away."

"Don't go to any trouble in my—" Pike began, but the pain lancing through his hand as the man holding his left arm broke his little finger stopped him. He barely had time to catch his breath when the next finger was pressed back until it, too, broke.

"There," Iron Eagle said, "now you are equal to your friend. You are both brave men, allowing yourselves to be mutilated to save the others."

Iron Eagle bent over Pike and spoke into his ear, so that the white man could hear him through the waves of pain that were coursing through him.

"Would they do the same for you?"

"Probably . . . n-not," Pike said through his teeth. He was perspiring so badly that a river of sweat was forming at his feet.

"Then why must you?"

"It must be . . . a flaw in . . . my character."

Iron Eagle said something to his braves and Pike's arms were now bent behind his back.

"Perhaps we should skip the other fingers and go right to your arms, eh?"

"The choice is yours," Pike said, speaking a little better now. His fingers felt numb, and he was sure that he was in shock to some degree. "I'm sure I have very little to say about it."

Iron Eagle stared at Pike for a long time and Pike did his best to hold the other man's gaze, even while his eyes were watering.

Finally, Iron Eagle spoke to his men again. Pike didn't even bother trying to translate. He'd know what was said soon enough.

There was some maneuvering behind his back and he realized that both of his arms were now being held by one man. The other man came around in front of him and tugged down his trousers and underwear.

"Ah," Iron Eagle said, "I am sure you have pleasured many of your white women with such a thing."

Pike looked down at his "thing." He was surprised to see that he was semi-erect. It was either due to the cold, or the pain.

"Some squaws, as well," he couldn't help saying.

"I am sure you have," Iron Eagle said.

He made a quick motion to the free brave, who reached out and took hold of Pike's penis. The man squeezed the head and tugged on the organ, stretching it out.

Iron Eagle stepped in close and took out his knife.

"I hope you remember the last woman you bedded, white man," he said, touching the sharp edge of the knife to the underside of Pike's penis, "because she was your last."

John Candy was relieved when McConnell woke up. He dragged the man across the floor and wrapped him in the blanket. He recalled Bridger saying that the best thing for a man in shock was to keep him warm.

"Where's Pike?" McConnell asked.

"He hasn't come back yet."

"How—" McConnell said, then paused and tried again. "How long?"

"Half hour, maybe more," Candy said. "What did they do to you? Did they hurt you . . . a lot?"

"Beat on me a bit, and broke a couple of fingers," McConnell said. "Mostly they tried to scare me. I don't think they were really trying hard, this time."

"Why not?"

McConnell moved, cradling his injured hand.

"I think they're counting on us scaring each other."

"Well, you look pretty scary at the moment," Candy said. "You're white as a sheet."

"Shock," McConnell said, "it'll pass."

"What do you think they're doing to Pike?"

"Probably the same thing," McConnell said. "The chief'll talk to him—listen to this, kid."

"I'm listening."

"The chief'll talk to you first. He's older than the others, and real soft-spoken. He'll even sound like a nice guy. He'll ask you first, and when you refuse to answer he'll turn you over to Iron Eagle."

McConnell paused as his hand began to throb.

"Jesus, John," he said, "tear me off a piece of your shirt."

"My shirt?"

"A strip," McConnell said. "I want to bind my broken fingers together."

"I'll do it."

Candy tore off a strip and McConnell unwound the blanket so the younger man could wrap the strip around his damaged fingers, binding them together.

"Tighter," McConnell said.

"I'm sorry," Candy said when McConnell hissed and stiffened.

"That's okay, just finish it."

When Candy was done McConnell moved his hand back inside the blanket.

"What will Iron Eagle do?"

"Huh?"

"I said what will he do?"

"Oh, Iron Eagle?" McConnell said. "Well, he thinks he's real scary, let me tell you. Had one of his boys snap my fingers and smiled at me the whole time. What a sonofabitch he is. Jesus, I wish I had something to drink."

"Sorry, Skins," Candy said, "I can't help you."

"I know that, kid. I tell you, though, that Iron Eagle, there's a man who really enjoys his work. He must *really* be happy when he has a woman to torture."

McConnell was too much in shock to realize it, but he was doing just what the Crow wanted him to do.

He was scaring John Candy to death.

Chapter Seventeen

Pike looked down at his penis in a way he had never done before. Now that he was in danger of losing it, it seemed to mean much more to him than ever before.

"How many women have you pleasured with this?" Iron Eagle asked, running the tip of his blade up and down the underside.

Pike couldn't answer.

"Many, I would say," Iron Eagle continued. "Women like big men — *I* know this for a fact. Women must be very impressed with you."

Again, Pike had nothing to say.

"But I wonder . . ." Iron Eagle said, looking as if he *was* actually wondering. He said something to the brave who was still holding Pike's penis and the man reached down and cupped Pike's genitals.

"If I cut *this* off instead," Iron Eagle said, nudging his testicles with the knife "then you could keep *this* — " poking his penis again — "and it would be useless!"

The idea seemed to fascinate Iron Eagle.

"Look," Pike said, "if you're going to cut something then go ahead and *cut* it."

Iron Eagle stepped back and stared at Pike, then said something to the brave who was still cupping the white man's genitals. The brave removed his hand, stood up and moved away. The brave behind Pike straightened him up painfully, and Iron Eagle kicked him in the genitals.

Pike saw bright lights and desperately tried to fall, but the brave behind him would not allow it. For a moment he was stunned, breathless, and then the pain set in and his eyes began to water again.

Iron Eagle moved close to him, whispering into his ear, "Now you truly do wish that I would cut it off, don't you?"

Iron Eagle said something in Crow and the brave behind Pike finally released him. Pike fell to the ground face first, right in front of the fire, landing on his broken fingers. The pain in his hand rivaled the pain in his groin. He thought he could hear voices around him, but he wasn't sure. They sounded so far away, fading more and more, until they—and everything else—was gone . . .

Pike came to with a start. He thought he was drowning, then realized that someone had thrown water into his face. He rolled onto his back and remained still. The pain still pulsed in his groin and his hand, and he could feel the heat from the fire on his face.

"Get up, white man," Iron Eagle said, "we are not finished."

Pike rolled onto his side again, facing the fire, which was made up of large wooden branches. Iron Eagle might not have been finished, but he was.

He rolled onto his stomach, as if he were readying himself to rise to his feet. He slid his right hand over and grasped a stout branch by the end that was not yet burning. As he rose he brought the branch up with all his force, striking one of the braves on the butt of the jaw. As quickly as he could he swung it backhanded, striking the other brave on top of the head. Both went down and he turned to face Iron Eagle.

The young warrior was stunned by Pike's move,

which had caught him flatfooted. Now as he grabbed for his knife Pike jabbed him in the stomach with the lit end of the branch. Iron Eagle opened his mouth to cry out in pain, but Pike swung the branch again and Iron Eagle slumped to the floor with his two braves.

Pike dropped the branch to the ground and relieved the unconscious Iron Eagle of his knife. He moved onto the two braves and took their knives, as well.

He paused, then, to take stock of the situation. He was alone, injured, armed with three knives and standing in a lodge in the center of the Crow camp. He doubted that in his present condition he could stand against one more brave, let alone the entire camp. He had to find the lodge where McConnell and Candy were still being held and free them. It did occur to him that he could escape alone, and probably with much more ease, but he pushed that thought aside. There was no way he could leave Skins McConnell behind to pay for his handiwork — and he was sure that when Iron Eagle awoke he would have McConnell and Candy killed to pay for Pike's escape.

He moved to the entrance of the lodge and peered outside. He had neither the time nor the material to tie the three Indians up, so he knew he was going to have to act quickly, before they awoke.

The grounds outside were still deserted, but it wouldn't be long before the camp stirred for the day. He slipped from the lodge and hurried across the grounds to the other side. He hadn't the time to slink from lodge to lodge carefully. His only course of action was to throw caution to the wind.

He moved quickly until he came within sight of the lodge he and his friends were being held in. There was a brave on guard in front of it, and he seemed alert. Pike was going to have to take him quickly and quietly.

He moved around behind the lodge and set two of the knives he carried aside. Slowly, he moved around the lodge until he could see the brave. He could either draw the brave to him or leap out at him. Either way he was going to have to overcome him quickly. The broken fingers on his left hand were swollen, making the hand unwieldy. A lengthy fight would work against him, and against their escape.

He decided to move out against the brave and leaped forward. The brave heard him and turned, reaching for his own knife. Pike crashed into him with his shoulder and fell to the ground with him beneath him. The knife was between them, and the edge bit deep and cut, bringing forth a torrent of blood. Pike fixed his injured hand over the brave's mouth to quiet his death cries until he lay still and dead.

Pike got to his feet and grabbed the brave beneath an arm. He dragged him to the entrance of the lodge and dropped him.

"Candy!" he hissed. He didn't call for McConnell because he felt that Skins had to be in worse shape than he was. "Candy!"

"Wha—" Candy said, moving to the flap. "Pike?"

"Help me."

Candy stepped outside and stared down at the fallen brave.

"Stop gawking and drag him inside. I don't want him to be seen."

Candy grabbed the brave beneath the arms and dragged him into the lodge, Pike following. Inside McConnell rose to his feet as they entered and reached with his good hand to help.

"How are you, Skins?" Pike asked his friend.

"I'll live, Jack. And you?" McConnell looked at his friend's hand. "I see you went through much the same. Iron Eagle must not have much imagination."

Pike thought about Iron Eagle's knife against his genitals and said, "Remind me to tell you about it some time."

McConnell looked again at Pike's swollen hand and said, "Let's bind those fingers. Flopping around like that they'll cause too much pain."

"There's no time," Pike said. "Let's move now!"

"Where?" Candy asked.

"Away," Pike said.

"We'll freeze!" Candy said.

Pike opened his mouth to argue, then closed it. He looked at McConnell, who shrugged.

"He's right, damn it!" Pike said. "We'll need some blankets."

"And horses," McConnell said.

Pike turned to face Candy and said, "Behind this lodge there are two knives on the ground. Get them and we'll figure out a way to get what we need without rousing the entire camp."

As Candy left McConnell said, "Let's get that hand bound, then."

Chapter Eighteen

They decided to go directly to where the Indian ponies were picketed. There they would find the blankets they needed, as well as the horses.

"The blankets may smell but they'll keep us warm," Pike said.

"A horse blanket sounds good to me," McConnell said.

Pike looked directly at John Candy when he said, "We'll have to move quickly and quietly."

"You lead and I'll follow, Pike," Candy said, "no questions asked."

Pike looked at McConnell and said, "That'll be the day."

They left the lodge and moved swiftly through the camp. As Pike was passing one lodge the flap was thrown back. A brave stepped out, sleep still in his eyes, and Pike planted his knife in the man's chest. Candy hurried forward and helped him lower the man to the ground inside his lodge. Pike was glad to see that there was no squaw present, or they would have had to kill her to.

"Let's move on," Pike said.

They continued on to where the horses were picketed and picked out three. They did not have time to find the same three they had ridden in on, nor to look for their weapons. They were going to have to ride out armed only with the knives they had.

"Can you ride bareback?" Pike asked Candy.

"Of course," Candy said. Pike saw the expression on the man's face, and doubted it, but said nothing.

"Fetch the blankets," Pike said to Candy. "Skins and I will free the other horses."

Candy collected as many blankets as he could carry. He hurried to the three ponies they had chosen and covered each with a blanket. While McConnell and Pike freed the other ponies Candy used his knife to convert three blankets into ponchos by cutting a hole in each.

"Here," he said as Pike and McConnell approached their animals. He helped them each to slip into their ponchos without jarring their injured hands.

"Good thinking, John," Pike said.

Candy accepted the compliment in silence.

"Let's get mounted up and get out of here," McConnell said.

Candy mounted easily while Pike and McConnell favored their injured hands.

As quietly as they could they urged the other horses to run off. Some were stubborn and Pike actually had to use his horse to push them physically.

"Let's go, let's go," he told the others.

As they rode away from the camp Pike doubted that they'd have much of a head start. Iron Eagle and the others were bound to wake soon, or someone would notice that the horses were gone.

What chance would they have, armed as badly as they were, with no supplies, of reaching Bridger's camp without being captured once again?

What chance? A better chance than they had as prisoners of Iron Eagle and a chief who called himself "The Bold."

Iron Eagle moaned and rolled over. His elbow came into contact with the fire and he jerked it away. The flesh of his abdomen burned, but he ignored it and got to his feet. He tried to rouse the other two braves, but one of them was dead, his head at an odd angle.

He turned to the other brave and pushed him.

"Fool!" he said. "Rouse the camp."

The brave stumbled from the lodge and began to run through camp, shouting.

Iron Eagle hurried to the lodge where the white men were being held, but all he found was another dead Crow brave. When he came out he found himself face to face with "The Bold."

"They are gone?" the chief asked. It was clear that he already knew the answer.

"They are gone."

"The Bold" cast a critical eye over Iron Eagle. He saw the burn on his abdomen and the bruise high on his forehead, over his left eye.

"The leader?"

Iron Eagle nodded.

"He must be very good," the chief said. "How many did he kill?"

"Two," Iron Eagle said, growing uncomfortable beneath his chief's gaze. "He caught us by surprise."

"I am not used to hearing excuses from you," the chief said.

At that point a brave came running up to them.

"What is it?" Iron Eagle asked, testily.

"The horses, they are gone."

The chief nodded, as if that were something he had expected.

"You will have to catch all the horses before you can bring the white men back."

"We will," Iron Eagle said. "They have no food, no weapons and no shelter. They will probably freeze to death before we catch up to them."

"I hope not," "The Bold" said to Iron Eagle, "for your sake."

Chapter Nineteen

Pike, McConnell, and John Candy rode as long as they dared push the horses, trying to put as many miles between them and the Crow as they could without killing the animals and themselves.

"We'll stay here about an hour," Pike said as they dismounted.

"Can I build a fire?" Candy asked.

"Why not?" Pike asked. "The Crow might smell it, but without it we'll freeze to death. I'll set a snare and see if I can't catch something to eat."

He came back sometime later with a scrawny rabbit which had been half dead itself when it stepped into his snare. They huddled around the fire in their makeshift ponchos, ate the meat and sucked the bones.

"Sorry I couldn't put on a better meal for you boys," Pike said.

"Are you kidding?" McConnell said. "That was mighty fine eatin', Pike."

"How are you fellas holding up?" Candy asked. "Your hands, I mean."

Pike looked at his and said, "Throbs some, but I'll survive."

"Me, too," McConnell said. "Least ways this *hand* won't kill me."

"Those Crow might, though," Pike said, "so we'd better get moving."

"I know you hate questions, Pike," Candy said, "but what kind of a chance do we have? Of avoiding them, I mean, and getting back to camp?"

"Not much, John," Pike said. "With rifles, and supplies maybe, but outfitted the way we are our chances are very slim."

"Then we'll die out here?"

"Most likely," Pike said. "Or we could let them catch us and die back there."

"Not much of a choice," Candy said.

"At least we've got one," Pike said. "That's more than we had back at that camp."

"He's right, John," McConnell said.

"I know he is," Candy said. "I just always thought I'd have more choices than where to die."

"You did," Pike said. "You chose to live in the mountains. Well, dying's part of living up here. If you didn't know that before, you know it now."

Candy digested that for a moment and then said, "Well, I guess we'd better get moving."

Iron Eagle looked down from his horse at the cold campfire and the scattered bones of what must have been a very small rabbit.

"If that is all the game they have been able to find they will be at least half dead by now."

Great Buffalo said, "If we do not bring them back, Iron Eagle, 'The Bold' will have our heads."

"We will bring them back," Iron Eagle said. "Their leader is a survivor. He will live." He touched the bruise over his eye and said, "I have much to pay him back for. He will live."

They camped for the night, huddling beneath their ponchos and blankets around a fire.

"Should we set a watch?" Candy asked.

"No need," Pike said. "If the Crow do come up on us there's no way we can fight them off. We might as well all get as much rest as possible."

They couldn't come up with any game for dinner, so they settled for some roots they were able to dig up.

"We get closer to the Yellowstone," Pike said, "we'll be able to find some game."

"Something we can get close to and kill with a knife?" Candy asked.

"No," Pike said, "something I'll just have to set a bigger snare for, is all."

"What I wouldn't give for some hot coffee," McConnell said.

"Be a while before we get anywhere near hot coffee," Pike said.

"I know," McConnell said, "but I can dream about it, can't I?"

"Sure can," Pike said, and added to himself, as long as we're alive.

In the morning when Pike woke he felt a moment of panic. It was as if he couldn't move, as if he were frozen solid. With a monumental effort he managed to sit up and looked around him. McConnell and Candy were still asleep — at least, he *hoped* they were asleep and not frozen solid. He leaned closer to them and saw that they *were*, in fact, alive and breathing.

He stood up, grabbed a pot and filled it with snow, then put it on the fire to boil. When it started to boil he removed it from the fire and allowed it to cool to a certain extent. It was still hot when he put his hands into it and put his hands to his face. There was a moment of warmth, and then the breeze touched his wet face and he knew that what he was trying just wasn't going to work. Even if he had a bathtub full of hot water, he would only be warm as long as he stayed in it, and as long as the water stayed hot.

He left the pot there, to give McConnell and Candy the option of using it, and woke them up.

"Jesus," McConnell said, "it's fuckin' cold."

Pike knew that McConnell was feeling the cold, because he didn't usually talk like that.

"I know," Pike said. "I don't need to be reminded."

John Candy sat up and shivered.

"What's that?" he asked, looking at the pot.

"Warm water," Pike said. "I thought it might help."

"Did it?" Candy asked.

"No."

"Then the hell with it," McConnell said. "Let's get moving."

Pike dumped the water out of the pot onto the fire and they broke camp.

When they were mounted Candy looked down at the doused campfire and said, "We're leaving them a trail a blind man could follow."

"We need the fire," Pike said. "Without it we would be dead men."

Secretly they all had the fear that they already were dead men, they just didn't have the sense to lie down and die.

How, they were all thinking, could they possibly outrun a band of angry — *angry* — Crow Indians when they were so poorly outfitted for it?

"You know what?" Pike said as they were riding.

"What?" McConnell asked.

"We're gonna fool 'em."

"Fool who?"

"The Indians."

"How are we gonna do that?" McConnell asked.

"We're going to make it."

"We are?"

"Yes," Pike said, nodding, "we are."

McConnell looked at John Candy, who simply shrugged and said, "No questions from me."

McConnell looked back at Pike and said, "That's a

sign. Now I know we're going to make it."

"There's one way I know we can make it," Pike said to both of them.

"How?" Candy asked.

"Make a bet."

"What?" he asked.

"Make a bet," McConnell said.

"You guys are crazy."

"No, we're not," Pike said. "We each hate to lose a bet."

"So, if we make a bet," McConnell said, "what would it be?"

"Well," Pike said, "if we do make it to the camp I get to sleep with both of the women Bridger supplied to us."

"We're talking about Jeanna and Donna?"

"Right."

"Don't they have anything to say about it?" McConnell asked.

"They're not out here with us," Pike said.

"Right," McConnell said. "Okay, so if we make it back, I get both women."

"And if we don't get back?" Pike said.

"Well then," McConnell said, *"you* get both women."

Pike grinned, put out his hand and said, "Then it's a bet."

"If we shake hands," McConnell said, "our hands will stick together."

Pike leaned over and he and McConnell bumped elbows.

"You guys are really crazy," John Candy said.

"You want in on this bet?" Pike asked.

"Of course," Candy said.

"Okay," Pike said, "you can have half my action."

"Oh no," Candy said, "I want half of Skins' action."

McConnell made a show of thinking about it and then said, "Okay, kid, if you think you can handle it."

Maybe they were all crazy, but for some reason they all suddenly felt a lot better — not about their chances of survival, they simply felt better.

Bridger had a bad feeling.

He sat in front of his tent, warming his hands by the fire, and he was worried about Pike, McConnell, and John Candy. They had been gone too long. He felt a fool, now, for even sending them out there. True, it had been Pike's suggestion, but that didn't mean that Bridger had to take it. No matter how much respect Bridger had for Pike, even Jack Pike had to be wrong once in a while.

Maybe his biggest mistake had been saddling Pike and McConnell with a green kid like John Candy. Actually, Candy was twenty-five, and wasn't really a kid, but in terms of experience he was. It was possible that having Candy along had caused Pike and McConnell more difficulty than Bridger had suspected. If he had left Pike and McConnell alone, maybe they'd be back by now.

Maybe they were all dead.

And maybe he was thinking about too damn many "maybes." He had a camp full of people here that he was responsible for, he couldn't sit around worrying about three men who were capable of taking care of themselves.

He'd have to stop thinking about them.

Sure, he thought, I'll stop thinking about them when they get back, and not before.

Chapter Twenty

The good feeling the three men had generated with their bantering faded fairly quickly. They rode along single file, huddled in their ponchos, heads down as they rode into the wind, chilled to the bone and aware of the smell of rain in the air.

As if things could get worse McConnell suddenly became aware that something was wrong with his mount. He barely had time to leap free before the animal keeled over. A little slower and he would have been pinned beneath the animal's great weight.

Pike dismounted quickly and ran to his friend's side.

"You all right?"

"Fine," McConnell said, "but the horse . . ."

They both moved to the animal, who was still breathing, but lying very still.

"What's wrong with him?" Pike asked.

McConnell checked the animal over as thoroughly as he could.

"I can't see a damned *thing* wrong with him," McConnell said. "He just keeled over."

"Maybe he was just ready to pack it in," John Candy offered, "like the rest of us."

"Stow that talk, boy," Pike said, giving Candy a hard look. "You may be ready to quit, but I sure as hell ain't. Understand?"

Candy looked away from Pike's glare.

"Come on, Pike," McConnell said in low tones, "leave the kid—"

"He's not a kid, Skins," Pike said, "and even if he was he should have grown up a little in the past few days. If he's ready to quit, he's not taking me with him."

McConnell gave his attention to the horse, stroking the animal's neck.

"He's a goner," he said.

"You want me to take care of it?" Pike asked.

"No, I'll do it."

Pike turned away as McConnell took out his knife and quickly slit the animal's throat. He wasn't quick enough to avoid getting blood on his hands, and it was so warm that he was momentarily tempted to leave his hands there. The animal shuddered for a moment, its eyes widening, and then lay still and stopped breathing.

"Skins—"

"I know, Pike," McConnell said.

He used the knife to butcher some meat from the animal. They could cook it up when they stopped to make camp. They had both eaten horse and mule before when they'd had to, and this was certainly a situation where they had to. They needed the nourishment if they were going to have any chance of making it.

Pike mounted up, turned his horse and reached his hand down to his friend. They had nothing to wrap the meat in, so McConnell just held it close to him, perversely enjoying the warmth it still held.

That warmth wouldn't last, though.

Not very long.

110

Iron Eagle stared down at the butchered pony.

"They steal our ponies and then eat them," Great Buffalo said with disgust.

"It will strengthen them," Iron Eagle said. "They are not fools."

"We will catch them and we will butcher them," Great Buffalo said, with feeling.

"Yes," Iron Eagle said, "we will."

Even with the meat in their bellies, Iron Eagle knew that the white men would not be able to avoid them for much longer. His only concern was that the cold would get them first. He wanted to bring at least one of them back to camp alive in order to save face before "The Bold," and before his men.

And the one he wanted was the big one, Pike. The man had surprised them in his own lodge, made a fool out of him, and for that he would pay dearly. He looked down at the butchered horse again and knew that he would soon be looking down at Pike, who would be in that same position.

After he told them what they wanted to know.

"I can't believe I'm eating this," Candy said, chewing on some of the horse meat.

"You'll find that you'll eat anything to survive," McConnell said. "Pike and I have eaten horse, mule, snake, dog, whatever we could catch."

"Pack rat," Pike said. "Remember that time all we could catch was a pack rat?"

"Uh!" Candy said, but that didn't stop him from popping another piece of the hot, gamey meat into his mouth and chewing enthusiastically. It was the first warm meat they'd eaten since before they were

111

captured.

"The Crow are gonna smell this, you know," McConnell said. "They're upwind of us."

"That's all right," Pike said. "They would have found the dead horse by now."

Candy stopped chewing and stared at Pike.

"You think they're that close behind us?"

McConnell was the one who answered.

"That close," he said, "and getting closer all the time."

Candy thought about it and said, "At this rate they'll be on us in no time."

"Well," McConnell said, "we have a choice."

"Like what?" Candy asked.

"We can let them kill us, or . . ."

"You mean, kill ourselves?" Candy asked, aghast.

"It's just a notion," McConnell said.

"Let's face it," Pike said. "When they catch us this time, what they did to us last time will seem like a game. This time one of us is going to talk— and tell the truth!"

"You mean me!" Candy said, bitterly.

"I mean any one of us," Pike said, testily. "Don't be reading into what I'm saying!"

"So the answer is to kill ourselves?" Candy asked. "With one of these?"

"It would assure that the people in the camp would be safe, at least for a while longer."

"Why don't we just go ahead and tell the Crow how many men are in camp?" Candy asked. "When they know that they're sure to leave it alone."

"They'd still kill us," McConnell said.

"And it wouldn't necessarily work that way," Pike said. "They might just go and get some more help and then attack the camp."

"I still can't see killing myself," Candy said.

"That's all right," Pike said, putting a piece of meat into his mouth, "one of us could always do it for you."

Candy gave Pike a quick look and said. "If that's a joke, it's in poor taste."

Pike just stared at the younger man, who was left to wonder if it *was* a joke.

When they camped for the night Pike was still thinking about what they had talked about that afternoon. Even taking into account what he had said to John Candy, he wondered if *he* himself would be able to commit suicide for the benefit of others. It was certainly an act that would be against his nature—against anyone's nature for that matter, but especially for him. He was a man who enjoyed life to the fullest, who would fight to the very end for just a second more of it.

There had to be another way, and if there was, by God, he was going to think of it.

When he woke in the morning, Pike knew that they'd never be able to survive another night out here, unless they found some way to keep warm.

"Skins," he said, nudging his friend. When McConnell didn't move Pike pushed him harder and shouted, "Skins, come on!"

He straddled his friend and slapped his face several times until his eyes opened.

"Come on, sit up!" he shouted, pulling McConnell by the front of his poncho.

"Wha—what's wrong?" McConnell asked, blearily.

"You wouldn't wake up," Pike said. "Are you

awake now?"

"I'm awake," McConnell said, rubbing his face, "I'm damned cold, but I'm awake."

Pike left McConnell to his own devices and moved on to where John Candy was lying. He repeated the process with Candy, slapping him until he woke and then hauling him into a seated position.

"Are you all right?" Pike said.

"Yeah, I am now," Candy said. "It was like I was . . . dreaming, or something. I could hear you calling me, but I couldn't move."

"We're going to have to find some way to keep warm," Pike said, "or I'm going to win a bet."

McConnell got to his feet and then Candy stood up, staggered and fell against Pike, who caught him and held him up.

"What's the matter?"

Candy looked at Pike with panic in his eyes, "I don't know. I can't feel my feet."

"All right," Pike said, "sit back down. I'll get your horse for you."

He lowered Candy back into a seated position and turned to McConnell. The two of them walked to where the two horses were standing.

"What is it?" McConnell asked.

"It must be frostbite," Pike said, "and there's nothing we can do about it out here. We'll just have to get him up on his horse and keep moving."

"You know," McConnell said, "If you and I keep riding this animal double he's not going to last very long."

"I know," Pike said. "You ride, and I'll walk and lead Candy's horse."

"We'll alternate," McConnell said. He held up his injured hand and said, "After all, we're both in the

114

same shape."

"All right," Pike said. "Let's get him up on his horse and get going."

Chapter Twenty-one

Bridger was getting fidgety.

"What are you gonna do?" Barry Bonds asked.

Bridger looked at Bonds, who was one of the old timers in camp. The man was correct in assuming that Bridger was preparing himself to make a move.

"I'll have to go out and find them, Barry."

"Bull!" Bonds said. "You cain't go out there and leave all these people here without a leader. That's just plumb crazy."

"You'll be here," Bridger said, "and Coleman, and Johnson. None of you needs me to hold your hands."

"That may be true," Bonds said, "maybe we don't, but the rest of these people sure do. They only came out here because they were following you. You ride out of here and how do you think they're gonna feel."

"Look, Barry—"

"Hell," Bonds said, not letting Bridger get a word in, "how do you think they're gonna feel if you don't come back?"

Bridger remained silent, thinking that one over. He had to weigh the good of over two hundred people against the good of three.

"Well?" Bonds asked.

"Well, you old fart," Bridger said, "you're right,

damn your eyes."

"Look," Bonds said, "Pike and McConnell know what they're doing."

"I know," Bridger said, "but I'm sure the Crow know what they're doing, too."

"Well," Bonds said, "I guess we'll just have to see who knows best."

"Yeah," Bridger said, "I guess we will."

It was the only decision he could possibly make, but that didn't mean it sat well with him.

"Look out!"

It was McConnell who shouted and Pike turned and saw that the horse John Candy was riding had stumbled and was falling forward. All Pike could do was duck out of the way and watch as the horse went to his knees and Candy was flying over the horse's head.

Candy landed on the hardpacked ground and the horse, having gone to both knees, then keeled over heavily onto its side.

McConnell dismounted and ran to Pike.

"Are you all right?"

"I'm fine," Pike said, from his knees. He wanted to get up but he was too cold. It felt as if his legs were two blocks of ice.

"Check the kid," he said to McConnell.

McConnell nodded and ran to see to John Candy, who had not moved since being thrown.

Pike slowly got to his feet and hobbled over to where the horse lay. It was clear to him before he even crouched over the animal that it was dead. He knew he should butcher the animal for the meat, but he wondered if there was really any point to it.

He turned and saw McConnell approaching him.

"How is he?" he asked.

"He's dead, Jack," McConnell said, shaking his head.

"What?"

"He's got a broke neck," McConnell said. "Must have hit the ground head first and snapped it."

"Shit!" Pike swore.

"Yeah," McConnell said.

Neither man said anything for a few moments, as if they were observing a moment of silence for their fallen comrade.

"Now what?" McConnell said.

"The ground's too hard to bury him," Pike said. "We'll need his blanket, and his knife, and one of us can wear his shirt—"

"I don't want it."

Pike didn't much want it, either.

"Well, get his blanket, anyway. One of us will have to wear that. We can also share it when we camp. I'll try and get the horse's blanket."

McConnell went to relieve Candy's body of his homemade poncho while Pike knelt by the horse and pulled on the blanket. It was pinned beneath the animal, so he used his knife to cut as much of it away as he could, coming away with about half a blanket.

"I wish we could cover him up," McConnell said, as it began to rain.

"We don't have the time to figure something out," Pike said. "Put on his poncho."

As McConnell slipped it over his head Pike cut a slit in the half blanket he had taken from the horse and then slipped it over his head.

"Do we ride double?" McConnell asked.

The rain was falling hard now, and made so much noise that they had to yell to be heard.

119

"We'll have to," Pike said, "for as long and as far as we can."

"It'll kill him."

Pike nodded. He knew that, already. Once this pony dropped dead they'd have to walk until *they* did the same thing.

McConnell knew it, too.

Soaked to the skin despite the double thickness of blanket/ponchos they were now wearing, Pike and McConnell were colder than they could ever have imagined being. They didn't think they could have gotten any colder, but they were, thanks to the rain.

All hopes that they'd get a few miles out of the weary pony vanished when the animal stepped into a hole. Pike was astride and knew the animal was in trouble. He threw himself free and landed without injury. McConnell also scrambled away from the animal as it fell.

They pony had broken a leg, and it was Pike who slit this animal's throat, putting it out of its misery.

"Well, that's it," McConnell said, "end of the line, Pike. On foot we won't last an hour in this rain."

"I don't think we have to, Skins."

"Why not?"

Pike was looking past his friend and Skins turned to see what he was looking at.

There were half a dozen Crow braves, wrapped in blankets and sitting astride their ponies, watching them from a small rise. Right in front Pike recognized Iron Eagle.

"I don't think we have any more waiting to do, Skins," Pike said. "None at all."

Part Four
The Sham

Chapter Twenty-two

The Crow made camp and started several fires. Pike and McConnell were surprised at the treatment they received. The Indians did everything they could to keep the two white men warm, and comfortable, including extra blankets.

"I find this insulting," McConnell said.

"What?"

"They haven't even tied us up."

"Where would we go, Skins?" Pike said. "We've gotten as far as we're going to get, I think."

"Yeah," McConnell said, pulling the blankets closer around him. "Next time we escape, we're going to have to be a little better prepared."

"Definitely," Pike said.

Silently they watched the Indians move around camp. Iron Eagle sat across camp from them, wrapped in blankets, watching them.

"What do you think he's thinking about?" McConnell asked.

"He's probably trying to figure a different approach to try on us."

"Like breaking toes instead of fingers?"

"Maybe," Pike said, "and maybe it's giving us blankets and putting us by a nice warm fire."

"You think he's trying to soften us up before he tries again?" McConnell asked.

"I don't know what I think," Pike said. "The blankets and fire may be just a way to keep us alive until we get back to their camp."

"You think he's going to take us back to their camp?" McConnell asked. "Why not do what they got to do right here?"

"Look at them, Skins," Pike said.

McConnell looked and saw the Indians crouched around their fires, blankets drawn close around them.

"They're just as cold as we are," Pike said. "They want to get back to the warmth and comfort of their lodges."

"I guess you're right."

"And after what happened the first time," Pike continued, "their chief, 'The Bold', probably wants to question us personally."

McConnell looked across the camp at where Iron Eagle was sitting, staring at them. The brave's eyes never wavered.

"You think we're better off with the chief?" McConnell asked.

"You're looking at Iron Eagle now, Skins," Pike said, "what do you think?"

"I think we're in a lot of trouble, either way."

"Well then, there's only one thing we can do," Pike said.

"What's that?"

"Plan our next escape."

"You just said—"

"I know what I just said," Pike replied, cutting him off, "but if we go along with them peaceably they'll find a way to make us talk."

"Then why don't we just make a run for it now?"

"And do what?"

"Wait for them to cut us down."

"They won't, Skins," Pike said. "They'll cripple us, maybe, and haul us back to camp, anyway. Or maybe they'd kill one of us and take the other one back."

"What about what you said to Candy?"

"I said a lot of things to Candy, Skins," Pike said, "but you know me. Do you think I could commit suicide?"

"To save two hundred people?" McConnell said. "Pike, I think you'd do anything."

Pike looked at his friend for a long moment, then grinned.

"I don't know," he said, "maybe you're right. Maybe I could do it, but I'd have to be sure—*absolutely* sure—that there was no other way."

"Oh, I see," McConnell said. "You're saying that the situation would have to be hopeless."

"That's right," Pike said. "Hopeless."

"Well, tell me this," McConnell said, "what are we facing here right now if not a hopeless situation?"

Pike thought about that for a moment and then chose his words very carefully.

"I think what we have here is a . . . serious situation . . . a *very* serious situation."

"Serious," McConnell said.

"Yes."

"I tell you what," McConnell said. "I'd hate to see what you consider to be a hopeless situation."

"Don't worry," Pike said, "you'll be the first to know."

In the morning they were rudely awakened by a foot in each of their sides.

"Up!" a Crow brave said.

Pike rolled onto his side and started to push

123

himself to a seated position with his left hand. He jarred the broken fingers and pulled his hand to his chest.

"Are you all right?" McConnell said.

"Yeah," Pike said. "My hand is so numb I keep forgetting I've got broken fingers."

"I know how you feel," McConnell said.

"Up!" the brave said again.

"We're getting up," Pike said.

They both staggered to their feet. They were cold, but not as cold as they had been the other mornings since their escape.

"Move!" the brave said.

He pushed them ahead of him, toward a couple of ponies.

Iron Eagle came over to them as they reached the horses.

"Where are we going?" Pike asked.

"Back to our camp," Iron Eagle said. " 'The Bold' is waiting to . . . question you."

"Are his methods any better than yours?" Pike asked.

Iron Eagle stared hard at him.

"He will ask questions," Iron Eagle said. "If you do not answer them you will once again have to answer to me." Iron Eagle took a step closer, so that he was almost nose-to-nose with Pike. "You and I are not finished, white man. We are far from finished."

Pike stared back until McConnell nudged his arm, then he looked away.

"Get on the horses," Iron Eagle said to both of them. "We are leaving."

As Iron Eagle walked away McConnell said, "We don't gain anything by goading him."

"I know," Pike said, "but I don't know how much

longer we're going to live, Skins. Let me have whatever fun I have left."

Chapter Twenty-three

They rode for most of the day, not stopping to eat or to rest. Neither Pike nor McConnell spoke, to the braves or to each other. Each of them was thinking and watching, waiting for an opportunity to do . . . what? Escape again? And go where?

They were riding side-by-side most of the time, with braves all around them. More than once their eyes would meet and they'd each try to read what the other was thinking.

When they stopped for the night they were fed and supplied with blankets.

"I feel like I'm being fatted for the kill," McConnell said.

"We are," Pike said, "but what else can we do? We've got to keep our strength up."

"For what?"

"For whatever comes, Skins," Pike said. "For whatever comes."

When they rode back into the Crow camp they were once again looked upon with curiosity, but there was also anger on some of the faces.

There was no anger, however, on the face of the man known as "The Bold." His face was strangely serene as he watched them ride toward him.

When they reached the point where he was standing the chief looked at Iron Eagle and said, "Bring them inside."

With that he turned and entered his lodge.

"Get down," Iron Eagle said, himself dismounting.

Pike and McConnell stepped down and a brave took their horses. Two other braves positioned themselves on either side of them.

"We are going inside," Iron Eagle said, fronting them. "If you are smart white men, and do not wish to die painfully, you will answer his questions."

"I'll tell you what your advice is worth to me, Iron Eagle—" Pike began, but suddenly there was a shot, and one of the Crow braves fell.

Pike and McConnell looked around frantically, hoping to see Bridger and some of his men.

"Blackfoot!" one of the Crow shouted.

"Take cover!" Iron Eagle yelled.

Pike saw the Blackfoot Indians, too many to count. They were on foot, firing their weapons and running into the Crow camp.

The Crow frantically scrambled for cover. For the moment, in the heat of battle, Pike and McConnell were forgotten.

"Pike," McConnell said.

"I know," Pike said. "Let's get the hell out of here."

They started to run across the camp, into the confusion, heading for the horses.

"Wait, wait," Pike said, grabbing McConnell's arm.

"What?"

"We'll need a gun, and some provisions."

"I'll get the gun and meet you at the horses," McConnell said.

"Right."

They split up.

McConnell turned and saw an armed Indian coming toward him. He wasn't sure if he was Crow or Blackfoot, but he charged the man, throwing himself at him bodily. They went down together and McConnell pummelled the red man into unconsciousness. He picked up the rifle and was busy removing the brave's powder horn and pouch when something hit him from behind.

The blow struck his back and he threw himself forward, away from whoever had struck him. He turned over and saw a brave standing over him with a knife. Quickly, he reversed the rifle and fired. The force of the shot propelled the brave away from him, where he fell onto his back.

He scrambled to his feet, grabbed whatever else he needed from the first Indian he had downed, and then started running toward the horses.

Pike realized he didn't know where to look for provisions. He also realized he was right in the middle of a firefight, and might have been shot at any moment by either side.

There were enough Indians running through camp—including women and children—to indicate that many of the lodges were empty. He decided to simply try some of them and see what he could find.

He had gone through two empty lodges and found some food, which he'd wrapped in a blanket. He also grabbed a couple of extra blankets. As he came out of the second lodge he saw a Blackfoot brave standing over a fallen Crow child, a little boy of about six. The Blackfoot was about to run the boy through with his knife, but the boy was not crying. He was simply staring at the man who was about to kill him.

Pike dropped the blanket he was holding and sprang at the Blackfoot, driving his shoulder into the man's abdomen. All the air escaped from the brave's lungs. The Blackfoot's hand was already coming down with the knife when Pike hit him, and the knife tore through his blanket poncho and opened a gash on his back.

Pike bore the brave to the ground, grabbed the hand that was holding the knife in both of his and snapped the wrist. The brave screamed, but the scream was cut off when Pike used his own knife on him.

Satisfied that the brave was dead, he turned to look at the boy, who had risen to a standing position. They looked at each other for a few moments, then the boy smiled, turned and ran off.

Pike reached for his blanket of food and holding it in his right hand and the bloody knife in the left, started running toward the horses.

McConnell was holding two horses ready when Pike got there.

"What the hell took you?" he demanded.

"I had a slight problem," Pike said. "I got some food and a knife, did you get a rifle?"

"I did," McConnell said, showing it to him.

"Then let's get out of here," Pike said, reaching for one of the horses.

"What happened to your back?"

"The guy I got the knife from didn't want to give

130

it to me."

"It looks like he gave it to you, all right."

"I have a suggestion."

"What?" McConnell asked.

"That we get out of here before the Crow and the Blackfoot forget that they hate each other and remember that they both hate white men?"

"Good idea."

The Crow must have been very busy with the Blackfoot following the attack on their camp, because Pike and McConnell never sensed the presence of the Crow on their trail. They had used the extra blankets to keep warm, the dried meat to survive until they found some game they could shoot with the stolen rifle.

When they finally rode into Jim Bridger's camp on the Yellowstone they were half asleep, half frozen, and half dead.

"Bridger!" Barry Bonds shouted.

Bridger came rushing out of his tent in time to see Barry Bonds catch Skins McConnell as he fell from his horse.

Bridger started to run but he didn't make it.

Pike fell from his horse and there was no one there to catch him.

Bridger knew that Pike would never believe he hadn't let him fall on purpose.

Chapter Twenty-four

When Pike awoke the first thing he noticed was the warmth. He didn't open his eyes. He frowned, but he didn't open his eyes. He was frowning because the warmth was not coming from any fire, or from blankets. What was it coming from? It was . . . on him, or over him. He felt it on his neck, on his chest, his legs . . .

Pike opened his eyes and looked down at the dark head on his chest.

Jeanna.

"Jeanna?"

Jeanna moved her head and looked up at him. She was naked, and so was he, and she was lying atop him.

"You are awake."

He looked at the ceiling of the tent for a moment, then back at her with a smile.

"More to the point," he said, "I'm alive."

"Yes, you are," she said, smiling back.

He frowned.

"The last thing I remember is being very cold."

"Well," she said, moving her legs slightly, "you are not cold, any more."

She kissed his chest and then rested her warm cheek on it.

He went back to sleep.

The second time he awoke he was alone. As he sat up the flap was thrown back on the tent and Jeanna entered. She was carrying a pan of water, and a cup of coffee.

"You are awake," she said, smiling, "and still alive."

"Thanks to you, I guess."

"I had to keep you warm."

"You did a fine job of it."

She put the pan down and handed him the coffee.

"What about Skins?"

"He is fine," Jeanna said. "He is with Donna."

"Well," Pike said, "I'm sure she's keeping him warm."

"Yes."

He frowned and put his hand to his head.

"What is it?"

"My head hurts," he said. "I have a bump."

"You fell off your horse as you rode in," she said, "you and your friend. Barry Bonds caught your friend before he hit the ground."

"And me?"

"There was no one near you," she said. "Bridger was running, but he could not reach you in time."

"I'm sure he tried his best," Pike said.

"I have some clothes for you," she said. "They belonged to the biggest man in camp."

"Who was that?"

"John Candy."

Pike stared at the dead man's clothes in her hand, then threw back his blanket and took them from her.

"He did not come back with you."

134

"No."

"He is dead?"

"Yes."

"I am sorry."

"So am I," he said, pulling on the pants. They were a little snug.

He used the pan of water she had brought him to wash his face and torso, and then pulled on Candy's shirt. It was a bit tight across the shoulders and chest.

He pulled on his own boots and finished the coffee.

There was a definite chill outside, but compared to what he had been through of late it was almost comfortable for Pike.

It was late afternoon. Pike walked across the camp to Bridger's tent.

"Hey, Bridger!" he shouted.

Bridger stuck his head out, smiled and said, "Wait a minute."

A moment later he reappeared, slipping his coat on.

"You're still alive, huh?" he said to Pike.

"No thanks to you," Pike said. "You let me fall on my head."

"Who told?" Bridger said. "Jeanna?"

"She said you tried your best."

"I did," Bridger said. "I just don't run as fast as I used to."

"Sure."

Bridger stared at Pike in feigned shock and said, "You don't really think I let you fall on your head on purpose, do you?"

"Of course not."

"Coffee?" Bridger asked. He had a pot on the fire in front of his tent.

"Yeah."

Bridger poured two cups and handed Pike one, and they sat across the fire from each other.

"I'm sorry about Candy," Pike said after a few moments.

"I know," Bridger said. "What happened?"

"His horse fell," Pike said. "He was thrown, and landed on his head. His neck broke."

"Jesus," Bridger said.

"He almost froze to death before that," Pike said. "We all did." He looked at Bridger and said, "Have you spoken to Skins yet?"

"No," Bridger said. "You're the first one up and about."

Pike looked down at his hand and realized for the first time that someone had rebandaged it. Probably Jeanna. She had done a good job. The fingers were straight, and immobile. They'd probably heal cleanly.

"Well then, I've got a story to tell you," he said to Bridger, "don't I . . ."

Bridger listened carefully as Pike told him everything that happened since they had left.

"They must have been watching us when you left," Bridger said. "Jesus, Pike, I'm sorry I sent you out there—"

"You didn't hold a gun to my head, Bridger," Pike said. "We all knew what we were risking."

"Candy didn't," Bridger said. "I sent him out there. He got killed . . . he could have gotten the two of you killed, and then I'd be responsible for all three of your deaths."

"You're not responsible for any of it, Bridger," Pike said. "Don't start doubting yourself. You've got too many people right here depending on you."

"I know, I know . . ." Bridger said. "Do you think

136

'The Bold' and his braves will come after us?"

Pike shrugged.

"That depends on how well they did with the Blackfeet," Pike said. "They still don't know what your strength is here."

"Maybe the Blackfeet will come after us," Bridger said.

"I think we'd better be prepared for anything, Bridger," Pike said.

"I'll put some watches up," Bridger said, standing up. He looked down at Pike and said, "I'm glad you and Skins made it, Pike."

"So are we," Pike said. "I'd better go and check on how he's doing."

"I'll walk that way with you."

Pike went to Donna's tent and called out, "Skins, are you alive in there."

He heard some muffled voices and then McConnell called out, "Give me a minute."

Pike folded his arms and waited, watching the activity in the camp. He knew from the looks of things that Bridger still had people moving around in shifts, to throw the Indians off. If Bridger's plans were working, the Indians — Crow or Blackfoot — would think there were about forty or fifty people in camp, not two hundred.

It suddenly struck Pike that this was probably not a wise front to put up. If the Indians finally convinced themselves that this was the truth, they'd come riding in. Granted, they'd be greeted by more guns than they were expecting — but there were bound to be casualties, even if they managed to fight the Indians off.

There was another way, a way to avoid any

casualties at all — if it worked.

Abruptly he became aware that McConnell was standing next to him.

"What are you thinking about?" McConnell asked.

"A plan," Pike said.

"Now you come up with a plan?"

"Did it ever occur to you that just because we made it back here doesn't mean we're out of trouble — especially not if 'The Bold' and Iron Eagle are mad enough to come after us."

"Well, maybe the Blackfeet took care of that problem for us."

"Bridger and I discussed that possibility," Pike said.

"And?"

"What's to keep them from riding on in here?"

"That's an encouraging thought."

"I think I have an idea," Pike said. "Let's go and talk to Bridger."

"Wait a minute," McConnell said, putting his hand on Pike's arm.

"What?" Pike saw a look of amusement come over his friend's face.

McConnell was frowning when he said, "Don't I remember something about a bet?"

"A bet?"

"Yeah," McConnell said, "we made a bet. Don't you remember?"

"No," Pike said, trying to keep from smiling, "I don't."

"It was your idea!" McConnell wasn't quite sure whether his friend was putting him on or not.

"It must have been the cold," Pike said. "It's either frozen your brain and given you visions, or it's frozen mine and given me amnesia."

138

"Well," McConnell said, looking back at the tent he had just come out of, "luckily I'm pretty satisfied with the present arrangement."

"Good," Pike said, "now let's go and find Bridger."

Chapter Twenty-five

They found Jim Bridger in the midst of about six men, probably setting up the watches.

"This will be day and night," he was saying. "If anyone doesn't think they can handle it, you'd better tell me now. I don't want to be overrun by Indians because someone couldn't keep awake."

He stopped and waited, but none of the six men spoke up.

"Good," Bridger said. "Work the watches out among yourselves. Two hours on and two hours off. Each man will get two two hour shifts during a twenty-four hour period. That way no one will fall asleep — I hope."

"You can count on us, Bridger," one of the men said, and the others nodded.

"Good," Bridger said. "Let me know what the rotation is to be."

He turned and saw Pike and McConnell watching him.

"Glad to see you up and around, Skins."

McConnell simply nodded his thanks.

"We'd like to talk to you, Jim," Pike said.

"About what?"

"I know what happened the last time I made a suggestion," Pike said, "but I've got another one."

"Well, what happened did happen to you. If you

want to make another suggestion, I'll listen — but first let's get some dinner and take it back to my tent."

They went to where several women were tending a few fires, accepted a wooden bowl each filled with vegetables and meat, and walked back to Bridger's tent.

"What's your suggestion?" Bridger asked them over the stew.

"I think we're taking the wrong course of action here by letting the Indians think we have fewer men than we really do."

"You want to show them how many men we really have?" Bridger asked.

"No."

"Then I don't think I understand."

"Neither do I," McConnell said.

"It's simple," Pike said. "Instead of convincing them that we have fewer men than we do, we convince them that we have more."

Pike watched as Bridger and McConnell both mulled over his suggestion.

"It could work," Bridger finally said. "We have two hundred and forty people. Of those there are probably a hundred able-bodied men who can shoot and fight. The rest are women and children. How would we do it?"

"Easily," Pike said. "Dress all of the women, and the larger boys and girls, as men and arm them all."

"We don't have enough weapons."

"You've got rifles and pistols in camp. Don't let anyone carry two weapons. Split them up, spread them as far as they'll go."

"That could work, Bridger," McConnell said.

142

"Yes," Bridger said, thoughtfully, "yes, it could, but if they're going to carry a weapon they should know how to use them."

"They can be taught," Pike said. "Skins and I could work with them."

"It would have to be done quietly, though," McConnell said. "No real shooting. It would attract attention. Someone watching might figure out what we were really doing."

"All we have to teach them is how to load, point and fire," Pike said. "That could be done without actually firing."

Bridger thought it over a moment longer, then said, "I like it, Pike. Damn it, why didn't I think of that?"

"It's the cold," McConnell said, sneaking a glance at Pike. "I understand it does something to your mind."

Bridger, Pike, and McConnell moved around the camp, informing people about the change in plan. They were told that the plan would be put into effect the following morning.

Several of the women — including Jeanna and Donna — were assigned to borrow men's clothing from around the camp. They were also told to make it look as though they were simply carrying laundry.

"You think the Crow know about laundry?" Donna asked Pike, smiling.

This was the first good look Pike had gotten at Donna, out in the light. Her blonde hair shone like spun gold, and her skin was like milk.

"It may be too late for this, Donna," Pike said,

"but borrow a hat and wear your hair under it."

"Why?" she asked. "You don't like blondes? Just blackhaired squaws?"

"The Indians haven't seen that many blondes, Donna," he said. "You might catch their fancy."

"You mean . . . they might try to . . . capture me?" she asked, her eyes going wide.

"They might," Pike said. "While you're at it, pass the word to the other longhaired women to keep it under their hats."

"I'll tell them," Donna said.

"What do you think?" McConnell asked.

"Very nice," Pike said, watching Donna walk away from them. "The Indians probably think the same thing." He turned to Bridger and asked, "Are there any other blonde women in camp?"

"No."

"Red?"

"No," Bridger said. "Mostly dark, some gray."

"Well, let's work on the longhaired ones," Pike said. "They can either tuck it under a hat, or get it cut."

"I'll have someone help Donna pass that word," Bridger said.

"McConnell and I will give indoor lessons on handling a rifle or pistol," Pike said. "We'll do it at night. What's your largest tent?"

"The supply tent," Bridger said, "larger now because we've gone through a lot of the supplies."

"All right," Pike said. "We'll start after dark, at half hour intervals. Anyone who wants to learn can come, but only six at a time. We don't want the Indians to start to wonder what's going on."

"We'll have to assume that they're still watching us," McConnell said, looking up at the mountains

144

around them, "whether they're Crow or Blackfoot."

"Right," Bridger said.

"By tomorrow," Pike said, "this camp is going to look like an armed fort."

"Without the walls," Bridger said.

"What I wouldn't give for some walls right now," McConnell said.

"Are you arming those guards?" Pike asked.

"Yes," Bridger said. "I've also decided to have them stand watch in twos, which will put them in four hour shifts."

"That's probably wise," Pike said. "Well, we'd better get set up."

"How?" McConnell said. "We just have to wait until dark until our pupils come."

"In case you don't remember, Skins," Pike said, "you and I don't own any weapons, any more."

"That's right," McConnell said. "It's a good thing I'm not the type who becomes emotionally attached to his weapons."

"I can help you with this," Bridger said. "I've got an extra Sharps, and an extra pistol. You fellas can fight over who gets what."

"You take the Sharps, Jack," McConnell said, "I'm a better shot than you with a pistol."

Pike decided to accept the Sharps and not argue the point.

Chapter Twenty-six

They decided to set up "classes" in two different tents. Pike would demonstrate how to load and fire the rifle, and McConnell would do the same with the pistol. Pike took the supply tent while McConnell set up shop in Bridger's.

Pike was surprised at how many men came to his "class." He would have thought that all mountain men grew up with a rifle in their hand.

They continued to demonstrate the loading and firing of the weapons until four in the morning. When Pike's last class filed out, Jeanna stayed.

"How did I do?" she asked.

"You're a born markswoman," Pike said. "You didn't need this class, Jeanna. You know the front end of a gun from the back."

"I know."

"So why did you come?"

"I wanted to make sure when you were finished you would come back to my tent," she said, sheepishly.

"Did you think I wouldn't?" he asked.

"As I said," she replied, "I wanted to make sure."

"Well, you can walk me over there, then."

Jeanna put her arm through his and said, "That is what I intended to do."

The cold raised goose flesh on Jeanna's breasts, and Pike covered them with his hands. Her nipples felt like small stones against his palms. He enjoyed the moist sounds she made as she rode him up and down. He liked the sound their flesh made when it came together, and the smooth feel of her buttocks against his thighs . . .

He lifted her off him and reversed their position so that she was on her back.

"Pike, no . . ." she said, reaching for him. He kissed her breasts, nibbling the nipples until she moaned aloud, and then licked his way down to her navel and beyond.

When he nestled his face between her legs he was pleased with how warm she was. He was delighted with how wet she was, and began to lick her, moving his tongue over her in long, slow strokes.

"Oooh, yes Pike . . ." she groaned, taking his head in both of her hands.

As he took her clit into his mouth and lifted her buttocks from the blanket she began moving against him, finding the tempo of his tongue and matching it. He slid his hands beneath her, cupping her buttocks and taking her weight.

She took it for as long as she could and then she said, "Wait, wait, wait . . ." but he didn't. He felt her belly begin to tremble, a sure sign that she was about to explode, and he simply squeezed her ass and kept licking.

Suddenly she was writhing beneath him, moaning and thrashing about in a frenzy. He held her buttocks tightly in an attempt to keep her still, but he was only partially successful. He had to rise to his knees at one point to keep contact with her, and then when her movements began to slow he lifted himself over her and drove into her. As the heat of her engulfed him she lifted her legs and wrapped them around him. He got up onto his knees, still holding her buttocks, and began to drive into her that way. He liked being able to look down at her face. Her eyes were closed and she was biting her lips. He marveled at the fact that during sex the look on a woman's face was almost a look of pain, when he knew that what they were feeling—what Jeanna was feeling—was intense pleasure.

It made him wonder how far apart pleasure and pain really were.

McConnell looked down at Donna as her tongue moved over him, leaving behind wet, cold patches. She licked him the way a horse works at a salt lick, or a sugar cube, working her way down and down until she was biting his pubic hair, wetting it, rolling it around her tongue.

McConnell lifted his hips from the blanket as her tongue worked up and down the length of his penis. She had one hand wrapped around the base of him, and the other hand was teasing his testicles. Finally, he felt her mouth come down on him, hot and avid, and she began to suck him noisily. The sounds she was making served to excite him even more, and she became even noisier when he exploded and she fought to accommodate his entire emission.

She continued to work at him afterward, until he was hard again, and then she mounted him and drove herself down on him.

He had never before met a woman who liked to

be on top of a man as much as she did.

On top of him, all over him, Jesus, it was like she was covering him completely with her hair, her mouth, her skin, smothering him with all the pleasure her body could give him . . .

"I told the women today that they want all the women to cut their hair," Donna said to McConnell later.

"Either that or wear it under a hat."

"I don't know what to do, Skins," she said. "I like my hair long like this, don't you?"

Her hair was fanned out across his chest and he touched it with his hand.

"I love your hair, Donna."

"I've never worn it under a hat," she said. "Will it stay?"

"It will if you tuck it under right."

She kissed his neck and said, "Will you help me do it right, Skins? I don't want to cut my hair off."

"I'll help you, Donna," he said. "Now go to sleep."

She pressed her face against his shoulder and said, "When will you be leaving?"

"I don't know."

"Before the winter ends?"

"I'm . . . not sure."

"I would like to leave, Skins," she said. "I didn't know what I was getting into when I agreed to come. I want to leave before . . . before we all get . . . killed . . ."

"Go to sleep," he said, wanting to get off the subject of when he was leaving.

He liked her, but he didn't love her, and he certainly did not want to take her with him when he and Pike left.

Which, if he had his way, would be as soon as possible.

"Do you think they will come for us?" Jeanna asked Pike.

They were lying together now under layers of blankets, still naked so that they could take advantage of each other's warmth.

"I can't say for sure, Jeanna," he said. "I know the Crow chief was planning on it, but he didn't want to move until he knew our strength."

"What will he think of the strength we are going to show him?" she asked.

"It might deter him," Pike said.

"Might?"

"He could always get more men," Pike said.

"How long would that take?"

"I don't know," he said. He knew she wanted to hear something encouraging, and he was trying to think of something. "It could take him what's left of the winter, and by the time he got back we might be gone."

"You'll leave before then, won't you?" she asked. "I mean, you're not going to stay with us the rest of the winter, are you?"

"I don't think so," he said. "If Skins and I can get Bridger to part with a couple of horses we'll probably be on our way once we've got this little sham set up."

She snuggled closer to him and said, "I wish I could go with you."

"You could," he said slowly, "if you wanted to."

"You do not need a woman slowing you down,"

she said. "Besides, I think I know you by now, Jack Pike."

"What does that mean?"

"You like women."

"Is that a crime?"

"Not if you treat all the women you like the way you treat me," she said. "Not if you give them all as much pleasure as you've given me."

"Jeanna—"

"You are not for any one woman, Pike," she said. "I know that. That is why I would not force myself on you. I will stay here when you leave. I will be here for the next man who needs someplace warm to sleep."

"Jeanna—"

"Shh," she said. "Go to sleep. You will want to be up early to oversee your—what did you call it, sham?"

"Yes."

"I want to get up early, too."

"What for?"

"I want to cut my hair," she said.

"Jeanna," he said, "you don't have to do that?"

"Yes, I do," she said. "I want to set an example for the other women. If we try to keep our hair now, we may all lose it later, right?"

"You're a smart lady, Jeanna."

"Yes," she said, "maybe too smart . . . sometimes."

Chapter Twenty-seven

When Pike woke in the morning he was aware that Jeanna was not next to him. She couldn't have been gone long, though, because her warmth still lingered within the blankets. He wondered if she had gone to get him some coffee.

When he opened his eyes and sat up he saw that she had not left the tent at all. She was sitting across from him, huge tears falling from her eyes, rolling down her cheeks and dripping off her face.

She had hacked her hair short with a knife, and all of her lovely long, black hair was on the floor around her.

"Jeanna—"

She smiled at him through the tears.

"I did not think it would hurt so much," she said.

He knew she wasn't talking about physical pain. He threw aside the blankets and took her into his arms.

Pike left the tent after Jeanna had stopped crying. As he left she was pulling on some men's clothes which had been borrowed from the smallest man in camp. She was still going to have to fold the pants legs up.

Pike met McConnell outside Bridger's tent, and

they talked while waiting for Bridger to come out.

"How are you getting along with Jeanna?" McConnell asked.

"Fine," Pike said. "She's a fine girl. Do you know what she did this morning? She cut off all her hair, to set an example for the other women."

"Donna would never do that," McConnell said. "She wanted me to show her how to tuck her hair up under a hat this morning."

"I'm sure some of the women will cut their hair and some won't."

"She's not talking about, uh, leaving with you when you leave camp, is she?"

"No," Pike said. "She understands."

"I'm afraid Donna's gonna ask to go along."

"So," Pike said, "make it clear before then that she won't be going along."

"I will," McConnell said, with a worried frown. "I will."

Bridger came out at that point and Pike handed him a cup of coffee.

"We'll have to get the people milling about today," Pike said.

"I know," Bridger said, warming his hands around the cup. "I want to check with the watches, first."

"Skins and I will start."

"After this cup of coffee," McConnell said. "It's gonna be a cold one, today."

"Why should today be any different from any other day?" Pike asked, grimly.

Pike and McConnell went from tent to tent, reminding people to dress properly when they were moving around camp. Some of the women complained about the clothes they had to wear, but both men were blunt about it.

"When you're dead," they said, "you won't have to worry about the clothes you're wearing."

That usually shut them up.

By ten that morning the camp actually looked crowded. It was important, however, that as many people as possible looked busy, like they were doing something and not just milling about. Even the Indians would be able to tell that they were the victims of a sham if too many people were just wandering aimlessly about the camp.

Pike looked around and hoped that this show of strength would be enough to deter the bloodlust of a brave like Iron Eagle.

Iron Eagle looked down at the white man's camp and could not believe what he saw. Had more white men come to the Yellowstone to camp?

Great Buffalo, sitting his horse beside Iron Eagle, said, "Where did they all come from?"

"I do not know," Iron Eagle said. Something was wrong, but he did not know what.

"They could not just have . . . appeared," Great Buffalo said.

"No," Iron Eagle said. "They could not."

He had an idea.

"Come," he said, "we must go and talk to 'The Bold'."

He hoped that his chief would agree with his plan. If he did not, he would have to carry it out against the chief's wishes.

Something was not right, and he was going to find out what it was.

"What do you think?" Bridger asked Pike.

"Well," Pike said, "I wouldn't attack a camp as obviously well armed as this."

"Apparently," McConnell said.

"What?" Pike asked, and Bridger frowned.

"As apparently well armed as this one," McConnell said. "Look closely."

Pike and Bridger did just that, looked very closely. There were people carrying weapons who had obviously never carried them before. There were also a lot of people wearing ill-fitted clothes, whether they were too small or too large.

"Well," Pike said, "we might get away with it as long as nobody takes a really close look."

The three of them stood and watched for a few more moments before Bridger broke the silence.

"Maybe we should pull out."

"And go where?"

"Down along the Yellowstone, past Twenty-Five-Yard River to Rocky Fork."

Pike looked at Bridger.

"You've been thinking this over, haven't you?"

"I have," Bridger said.

Pike rubbed his jaw and studied the activity going on in camp.

"Why don't we wait a few days, Jim, see how this works out?"

"If we go, will you come with us?" Bridger asked. "I'd need you fellas on a trip like that."

Pike looked at McConnell, who shrugged, indicating the decision rested with his friend.

"Let's wait a few more days . . ." Pike said again.

"No," "The Bold" said.

"What?"

Iron Eagle could not believe his ears. Even though he was prepared to move without the chief's approval, he was surprised at not having gotten it.

"Why?"

"The Blackfeet did us damage, Iron Eagle," "The Bold" said.

"What has that to do with the white men?"

"We would do better to ally ourselves with them against the Blackfeet."

"Crow need no help to kill Blackfeet!" Iron Eagle said, stubbornly. "We killed those who attacked our camp."

"And they killed many of us," "The Bold" said. "We are weakened, Iron Eagle, and if what you say is true, the white men are more in strength than we believed."

"I cannot believe this," Iron Eagle said. "You would ally yourself with them?"

"To save my people," "The Bold" said, "I would ally myself with a devil if I had to."

"Bah!" Iron Eagle said, rising and moving to leave the chief's lodge.

"Iron Eagle!" "The Bold" barked.

The brave turned at the sound of his name and stared at the older man.

"Do not oppose me on this."

They stared at each other for a while longer, and then Iron Eagle left without further word.

Part Five
Truce

Chapter Twenty-eight

Bridger was awakened abruptly in the morning by Barry Bonds.

"What is it?" he demanded as Bonds shook him awake violently.

"We got company, Jim."

"Who?"

"Crow."

Bridger was instantly awake.

"What are they doing?"

"Nothing."

"Nothing?"

"They're just standing there," Bonds said, "waiting."

Bridger pulled on his trousers and asked, "Waiting for what?"

"Damned if I know."

"Shit," Bridger said, reaching for his shirt. "Wake Pike and McConnell."

"Right," Bonds said. As he turned to leave the tent Bridger called his name.

"Go easy," he told him. "We don't want it to look like we're panicking."

"Right," Bonds said, "easy."

He took a deep breath and then left the tent.

Pike's plan had been in effect for three days, and the people in camp were starting to think that maybe it was going to work.

To Pike, McConnell, and Bridger the half of their people still looked comical wearing clothing that was too big — and, in some cases, too small — and carrying around weapons they knew nothing about except what they had been hurriedly taught several nights before.

As Bridger finished dressing he wondered if the Crow had finally seen through their deception?

"Pike!"

Pike sat up, instantly alert, and stared at the head of Barry Bonds, which was sticking through the entrance of the tent.

"What is it?"

"Crow," Bonds said.

Pike tossed back his blankets. He wasn't aware that he had exposed one breast and hip of Jeanna's. Bonds, however, did notice.

"Bridger?"

"He's awake," Bonds said. "I'm waking McConnell next."

"All right," Pike said, reaching for his shorts. "Where are they?"

"North about twenty yards," Bonds said.

That close, Pike said to himself.

"All right," he said, "go, but —"

"I know," Bonds said, "go easy."

"What do they want?" Jeanna asked, pulling the blanket back over her.

"I don't know," Pike said, pulling on his shirt.

"Have they come to kill us?"

"If they had," Pike said, "I think we'd be into it by now."

160

"Maybe they figured out our trick?"

"Maybe," Pike said, "or maybe they're here to find out once and for all how many we are."

"Maybe they want to make friends," Jeanna said.

Pike was already heading out of the tent when she said that, and he stopped short and stared back at her.

"It is possible," she said, in self-defense.

"It is," he said, nodding. "Anything's possible."

They stared at each other for a few moments and then he said, "Stay inside," and left.

"Don't come outside," McConnell told Donna.

"What are you going to do?" she asked him as he dressed.

He stopped for a moment and said, "I don't know for sure. I guess we'll just have to see what they want."

"Be careful."

He gave her a hard stare and said again, "Don't come outside."

Outside McConnell saw both Pike and Bridger coming toward him. Bonds was standing outside of McConnell's tent, and they all converged there.

"There they are," Bonds said. "Like I said, just sittin' their horses and watching."

The other three men saw that he was correct. There was a group of Crow Indians, the exact number indeterminable at this distance, about twenty yards away. They were all mounted and they were all just standing still and watching the camp.

"Do you see Iron Eagle?" Pike asked McConnell.

"No, but I see 'The Bold,' right out there in front."

"Yeah, I see him."

"What do we do now?" Bonds asked.

"I'll have to go and see what they want," Bridger said. "Pike, will you come with me? He knows you."

"Let's go," Pike said.

Pike handed his Sharps to McConnell, and Bridger handed his to Bonds.

"Let's go and see what they want from us," Bridger said.

Pike and Bridger walked to the edge of camp and then suddenly a rider broke away from the main body of Indians and began riding toward them.

"That's 'The Bold'," Pike said.

Bridger nodded, and they kept walking. Eventually, when they had closed half the distance between them and the Crow, they stopped and waited for "The Bold" to reach them.

When the chief was within twenty feet of them he stopped his horse and dismounted. Pike was somewhat surprised that the man had come forward alone.

As he approached the two white men on foot Bridger said, "What do you count?"

"I think he's got about forty braves with him."

"He doesn't know how outnumbered he is."

"We don't know who else he's got nearby."

They stopped talking as "The Bold" reached them.

"You are Pike," he said.

"Yes."

"Is this your leader?"

"Yes," Pike said. "He is Bridger."

"Ah," the Crow chief said, "Casapy, the Blanket

162

Chief."

Bridger did not acknowledge his nickname, pronounced "Kash-sha-peece," which meant "fine cloth." Bridger's women had at one time sewed together yard wide strips of colorful cloth, the seams beaded with quills. It was a full dress raiment that he sometimes wore for parties, or just to show off.

"The Bold" had obviously heard of Bridger.

"Why have you come here?" Bridger asked.

"For peace."

Bridger's eyebrows went up.

"You have been watching us for a long time," he said, frankly. "As soon as you knew our strength you would have attacked us."

"This is true," "The Bold" said, "but things have changed."

"How?" Bridger asked.

"The Blackfoot have come," "The Bold" said. "They have attacked the Crow, and will attack you."

"We have fought the Blackfoot before," Bridger said.

"As have we," said "The Bold."

"What are you suggesting, then? A truce?"

"Yes."

"You want us to fight the Blackfoot together?"

"Not together," "The Bold" said, "but if we do not have to worry about each other, then we can concentrate on the Blackfoot."

"They have not bothered us."

"They will," "The Bold" said. "You know they will."

Bridger took a quick glance at Pike, who gave him a slight nod.

"How long would this truce last?" Bridger asked.

"As long as the cold," "The Bold" said. "When the

163

waters move again, the truce will be over."

"And we will be enemies again," Bridger said.

"Yes."

Bridger looked at Pike then, and said, "It is agreed, then."

"Agreed," "The Bold" said, nodding. He was turning to walk away when Pike spoke.

"Will your young bucks keep the peace?"

"They will," "The Bold" said. "I have given my word."

"Will Iron Eagle keep your word?" Pike asked.

There was a split second of hesitation, just enough for Pike to know that even "The Bold" wondered about that, himself.

"He will keep it," the chief said.

Pike remained silent, and "The Bold" remounted and rode back to his braves.

"What do you think?" Bridger said.

"Well, we know he's sincere," Pike said. "He's a chief, and an honorable man."

"And Iron Eagle?"

"He's young, and he's a hothead," Pike said. He looked at Bridger and said, "I wouldn't remove the watches just yet."

Chapter Twenty-nine

They kept up the deception for the remainder of the week, and at week's end met to discuss what their next move should be.

They were in front of Bridger's tent: Bridger, Pike, McConnell, Barry Bonds, and some of the other men from camp who had been with Bridger the longest.

"If we have a truce with the Indians," one man said, "we can go ahead and see the winter through here."

"We have a truce with the *Crow*," another man said. "What about the Blackfeet?"

"Maybe they won't come near us," the first man said.

"You want to take the chance?" the second man said.

A third man said, "Never mind the Blackfeet, can we trust the Crow to keep this truce?"

Bridger decided to answer that.

"Pike and I talked to their chief and we feel he was sincere. However, there are some of his braves who might not agree with him."

"What you're saying," Barry Bonds said, "is that we have an uneasy truce, at best."

Bridger smiled.

"That's exactly what I'm saying."

"Then I say let's move on," one of the other men said. "Let's get out of here now."

"I say we stay," someone said.

"Pike?" Bridger said. "What do you say?"

"My feeling is that it might be wise to start moving while we do have a truce with the Crow."

"Skins?" Bridger said.

"I agree."

"So do I," Bridger said.

"Don't we have any say?" asked the man who had been arguing to stay.

"Sure you do, Jeb," Bridger said. "Anyone who wants to stay behind can."

"Whataya mean stay behind?" Jeb said. "We came out here with you, Bridger."

"And agreed to abide by my leadership. Why are you questioning me now, Jeb?"

Jeb hesitated and then said, "All right. When you leave me and mine will be with you."

"When do we do this, Bridger?" a man named Carlton asked. "I mean, when do we strike camp?"

"In the morning," Bridger said, "just before first light."

"Are we being watched?" Jeb asked.

"Probably," Pike said.

"By who?" Jeb asked.

"It doesn't matter," McConnell said. "There are Crow and Blackfeet out there. We might as well assume we're being watched by either one, or both."

"And when they see us break camp what are they gonna do?" he asked.

"I guess we'll find that out tomorrow," Bridger said, "won't we, Jeb?"

When the others left to see to their belongings, Pike stayed behind and had a cup of coffee with

Bridger.

"I suggest we keep up our deception for a while, even while we're on the move," Pike said.

"I agree," Bridger said. He looked over at Pike and asked, "Tell me what you're most worried about?"

"Iron Eagle."

"Why?"

"He's a leader, Jim," Pike said. "What we can't possibly know is just how many braves he could get to follow him."

Bridger nodded.

"What's your big worry?" Pike asked.

"The Blackfeet," Bridger said. "If there are enough of them to push the Crow into this alliance, this truce, there must be a lot of them."

"I guess," Pike said. "Hopefully, we won't find out about any of this."

"Hopefully," Bridger said.

They finished their coffee in silence and then took another cup each.

"What are you and Skins going to do?" Bridger finally asked.

"Well, we've talked about it some," Pike said. "We figure if you're moving out anyway we might as well go along with you. There's no point in us going out on our own when we can travel with you."

"Alone you might go unnoticed by both the Crow and the Blackfeet," Bridger suggested.

"You think so?"

"Only because it's you and McConnell," Bridger said. "Sure, you fellas could avoid them."

"Maybe," Pike said. "I think we'll just stay with you for a while, if that's all right with you."

It was more than just all right with Bridger. He

felt that Pike and McConnell were only staying because they felt that Bridger needed them, and that was fine with him. He liked having two men as competent as this pair around.

"You know what?" Bridger said, after a moment.

"What?"

"I think next year I'll winter alone."

"That sounds like a wise decision," Pike said, nodding his head.

When Pike left Bridger he went back to his tent, where Jeanna was waiting.

"What was decided?"

"We'll be moving out in the morning."

"You and Skins?" she asked.

"All of us, Jeanna," he said, sitting on the blankets with her. "We'll all be moving out and traveling downriver."

"So you're coming with us?" she asked, happily.

"Until we reach a settlement, yes," Pike said. "Once everyone is safe, Skins and I will go our own way."

Jeanna ran her hands up Pike's back, kneeling behind him. She pressed her breasts and cheek against his broad back.

"I'm glad," she said. "We will be together a little while longer."

"Yes," Pike said, aware of her warmth even through their clothes, "a little while longer."

He turned and helped her out of her clothes, burying his face on her warmth. Her flesh was smooth and fragrant, her nipples hard as he bit on them.

She pulled his clothes from him and they fell

across the blankets together. Her hands encircled his engorged penis as he kissed her, his big hands roaming over her body until one hand came to rest between her legs. She was wet and his fingers made her even wetter, and when he entered her he was once again struck by the heat she carried inside of her, and by the heat she caused inside of him.

It was a wonder they didn't both burst into flames.

Later that night, after the camp had turned in, Pike slipped from the blankets, careful not to let any of the warmth escape. Naked, he stepped to the tent flap, pushed it aside and stepped outside. The cold struck him and he stiffened for a moment, then closed his eyes and experienced it as it washed over him. He wouldn't be able to stand it for too long, but for the few moments he stood there, he felt alive. He had been afraid that he'd lost this, that the time he'd spent running from the Crow, freezing with McConnell and poor John Candy had robbed him of this. He was very happy to find he had not lost it.

He loved the mountains, and you couldn't love them if you didn't like the cold.

He returned to the confines of the tent, took an extra blanket and wrapped it around himself. He did not want to get back beneath the blankets with Jeanna while his flesh was still cold. He sat there, watching her sleep, waiting for his body temperature to reach normal level so that he could crawl back under the covers with her.

Pike woke well before first light and got dressed.

"Stay asleep," he told Jeanna as she rolled from the blankets.

"There is much to do," she said, and also got dressed.

Outside he saw that he was not the first one up. Bridger was already up and about, and talking to the two men who had been on watch.

"Have they seen anything?" Pike asked as he reached Bridger.

"No," Bridger said, "but that doesn't mean they're not out there."

They both stared out into the darkness that still surrounded the camp.

"Well," Pike said, "what do you say we see how fast this camp can be broken down?"

"Let's do it," Bridger said.

Chapter Thirty

On the way down the Yellowstone Bridger decided to send some of the trappers to work along the tributaries. After all, hunting and trapping was still their prime reason for being where they were.

At one point Bridger had so many of the trappers and hunters out that he had twenty-five able-bodied men in their camp at the mouth of Twenty-Five-Yard-River.

Of course, they still had most of the women dressed as men, and from enough of a distance the deception was still working—or so it seemed.

They were also sending men to backtrack and see if they were being followed. Once or twice it was Pike and McConnell who rode the back trail, as they were doing now.

"You know, as sharp as our eyes might be," McConnell said, "if there are Crow or Blackfoot braves out there who don't want to be seen, we sure as hell ain't gonna see them."

"Well," Pike said, "they'll see us, and they'll know that we're looking for them."

"What do you think will happen with Iron Eagle?"

"I think we'll be seeing him again soon," Pike said. "He's not going to forget what I did to him in his lodge."

"You think he'll defy 'The Bold'?"

"I think you and I have both seen some Iron Eagles in our time, Skins," Pike said. "He'll do whatever he thinks is best for him to do."

"Well, maybe he won't get that many braves to follow him," McConnell said, hopefully.

"Maybe he won't," Pike said, but he didn't hold out much hope for that. There was usually no shortage of men ready and willing to follow the Iron Eagles of this world.

"Let's get back," Pike suggested.

On the way back McConnell asked, "What do you think of Bridger having so many men working the tributaries?"

Pike shrugged.

"Hey, that's what they're here for, Skins," Pike said. "I can't criticize Bridger for continuing to conduct business."

"I guess not."

They rode along in silence for a few moments and then Pike said, "How are things going with Donna?"

"She's still making noises about going with us when we leave Bridger."

"I hope you're being direct with her."

"As direct as I can," McConnell said, "while I still want to be kept warm at night."

"You're a terrible man, Skins."

"I know, I know."

They rode into the temporary camp and turned their horses over to someone before joining Bridger around the coffee pot.

"How does it look?" Bridger asked.

"Clear," Pike said, pouring himself a cup, "how else is it going to look?"

"Yeah, I know," Bridger said, sullenly, "if and

when they do come, they'll be on us before we know it."

"Maybe you shouldn't have so many of the men out, then," McConnell said.

Bridger gave him a sharp look, and then switched his gaze over to Pike.

"That what you think?"

"Skins is just making a suggestion, Jim," Pike said. "Nobody's criticizing you."

"Yeah," McConnell said, "I didn't mean anything by it, Bridger."

Bridger waved his hand and said, "Ah, I know you didn't, Skins. I think I'm just feeling a little guilty."

"Guilty?" Pike asked. "About what?"

"Bringing all these people out here to winter, exposing them to danger—"

"You didn't force any of these people to come with you," Pike said, interrupting him. "I don't know why you should feel guilty."

"Poor Candy—"

"He could have fallen off a horse anytime, Bridger," Pike said. "That's not your fault."

"Maybe," Bridger said, rubbing his hands over his face, "and maybe not. I know one thing, though."

"What's that?"

"After this the only person I'll be taking any responsibility for is myself."

"Well," Pike said, "I can't say I much blame you for that, but why don't you hold off making any decisions until you've been able to think all this through some place . . . warm, over a hot meal and a cold beer."

"Sure," Bridger said. He stood up and said, "I'm going to take a walk."

173

As Bridger walked away McConnell said, "I've never seen him like that, before. Bridger is usually in control of himself."

"He's human, just like the rest of us," Pike said. "He feels he's put the lives of over two hundred people in danger, and that he caused the death of at least one. He doesn't want anyone else to die."

McConnell looked around at the people who were in camp, sitting around fires, all bundled up, women feeding children, men looking around warily, nervously.

"They're all waiting for something to happen," McConnell said. "If we do get attacked, they're gonna panic. Some of them are gonna end up dead."

Pike looked around, pouring himself another cup of coffee.

"We get nearer Clark's Fork we won't be far from the Clark's Fork settlement," Pike said. "At that point these people will have more choices than they have now. They can keep following the river, they can go to the settlement, or they can move up into the mountains."

"You and I would go into the mountains," McConnell said, "but not these people."

"The Indians won't come that close to the settlement, so they'll be a lot safer than they are now, no matter what they decide."

"What about Bridger?" McConnell asked.

"He'll come out of it," Pike said, "once he realizes that none of this was his fault."

Iron Eagle had come up with a plan.

He and the braves who had chosen to follow him

had noticed the men working the river tributaries. For several days they had watched the men, and then Iron Eagle realized that there was a way he could show the white men that not all the Crow were like women, like "The Bold".

"We will show them how a true Crow warrior lives," he said to Great Buffalo.

"How?" Great Buffalo asked.

Iron Eagle laughed.

"Come," he said, "I will show them and you at the same time."

Pike and McConnell were both attracted by the sound of an approaching horse. They looked up and saw Barry Bonds ride into camp on the double, dismounting even before the horse had time to stop.

They stood up and caught him as he ran into them.

"What is it?" Pike asked. "What happened?"

"They're dead," Bonds said between gasps of breath.

"Who's dead?"

"Morley, Davidson, Wayne, two others," Bonds said. "We were working one of the tributaries together and we split up into twos. I went with Wayne, and then we split up. When I came back, he was dead."

"And the others?"

"I went looking for them, and they were dead too, all of them."

"Dead from what?" McConnell said.

"Indians."

"Crow or Blackfoot?" Pike asked.

"I didn't see the Indians," Bonds said, "just the

bodies of our people. They'd been mutilated."

Pike looked at McConnell and said, "Iron Eagle."

"What's going on?" Bridger asked.

Pike said to McConnell, "Get some coffee into him," and McConnell took Bonds with him.

"Five dead men," Pike said, watching Bridger's face carefully.

"Where?" Bridger asked. "How?"

Pike told him what Bonds had told him and McConnell, still watching the man's face for his reaction.

"Jesus," Bridger said, running one hand through his hair.

"What do you want to do, Jim?" Pike asked softly.

For a moment he thought Bridger had not heard him, but before he could repeat the question Bridger's eyes seemed to focus on him.

"Let's have Bonds take us to where the bodies are," Bridger said.

"Good idea," Pike said. "I'll have McConnell stay here with the others. He'll keep them calm."

"I'll get the horses," Bridger said.

Pike had been afraid that the news of not one but five more deaths would have five times the effect on Bridger that John Candy's death had. He'd watched his friend carefully, and except for a vacant moment in the eyes, Bridger seemed to be reacting fairly well.

He hoped that would continue to be the case.

Barry Bonds took Pike and Bridger to where he'd discovered the first of the bodies, and then on to the others.

"The ground is too hard to bury them," Bonds complained.

"Barry," Bridger said, "you'll come back with some men and collect them. Roll them up in blankets and bring them back to camp. We'll make an effort to bury them."

"All right," Bonds said.

"How many of them were married?" Pike asked.

"Two," Bonds said, "Davidson and Wayne. Wayne has two children, as well."

"I'll tell their wives," Bridger said.

Pike and Bridger examined the last two dead bodies—those of Davidson and Wayne—more closely than they had the others.

"These mutilations are meaningless," Pike pointed out.

"I know," Bridger said. "This is a message, is that what you're thinking?"

"It is," Pike said.

"From whom?"

"Iron Eagle."

"Not 'The Bold'?"

"No."

"Or the Blackfoot?"

"If the Blackfeet had mutilated these men, the injuries would have made more sense," Pike said.

"I agree," Bridger said. "Iron Eagle has taken it upon himself to defy his chief."

"So what do we do about it?" Pike asked.

Bridger stood up and moved toward his horse, taking the reins from Barry Bonds. Pike took a last look at the two dead men, and then followed.

When all three were mounted Bridger said, "I think maybe you and I should try and find 'The Bold' and let him know. What do you think?"

"I think that's certainly one solution to the problem."

"Do you have another?" Bridger asked.

"Not at the moment."

"Then for now," Bridger said, "we'll do it my way."

Chapter Thirty-one

They returned to camp and Bridger instructed Bonds to round up the men he would take with him to fetch the bodies.

As Bridger and Pike dismounted Jim Bridger said, "I'll go and talk to the widows."

"I'll see to getting us fresh horses and supplies," Pike said.

Pike gave the horses over to a young man to care for and then walked over to where McConnell was sitting by one of the fires.

"What's the verdict?" McConnell asked.

Pike hunkered down across from his friend and said, "I still think it's Iron Eagle."

"And how many braves?"

"The ground was too hard for any sign," Pike said. "If I had to guess, though, I'd say he didn't have nearly enough to come riding in here on us."

"Just enough to pick us off one or two at a time, eh?" McConnell asked.

"That's my guess," Pike said.

"So what are we going to do about it?"

"Bridger and I are going to try to find 'The Bold' and tell him that Iron Eagle has broken his truce."

"Why don't we just go out with twenty-five men and find Iron Eagle and his men?" McConnell said.

"That would leave the camp open for attack, if

not from Iron Eagle then from the Blackfeet."

"Ah, the Blackfeet," McConnell said. "That's right, we still could have them to contend with. Still, I don't like the idea of you and Bridger going out alone. I mean, look what happened to us when we tried it."

"Well, it's Bridger's idea," Pike said.

"And you don't want to argue with him?"

"It's not a bad one," Pike said. " 'The Bold' must be moving around with his people, either looking for the Blackfeet or trying to avoid them."

"What if you run into Iron Eagle and his men?"

"I guess we'll just have to be careful not to."

At that moment a woman's cry split the air, lingered a moment, and then died away.

"Bridger's breaking the news to the widows," Pike said.

"What am I supposed to do while you're out playing dodge the Indians?" McConnell asked.

"Keep these people moving, and keep them calm," Pike said. "You and Bonds will have to take care of that."

"Terrific," McConnell said. "Suddenly, *I'm* responsible for the lives of over two hundred people."

Pike clapped his friend on the shoulder and said, "It gives you a great feeling of power, doesn't it?"

McConnell gave his friend an expressionless stare as a reply, and Pike stood up.

"Bonds is going to take some men to collect the bodies."

"We'll try and find some place to bury them," McConnell said. "Maybe we can even chip through the ice of the river and bury them there."

"Whatever you have to do," Pike said, "but the most important thing is to keep the people from

180

panicking."

"I'll get them to pray together," McConnell said, "that should do it."

"Come on," Pike said, "help me get some supplies and a couple of fresh horses."

As they moved away from the fire they heard another woman cry out.

Bonds and his men were ready to leave before Pike and Bridger. In fact, Bridger was still with one of the dead men's widows when Bonds mounted up with six men and five extra horses.

"We'll be gone by the time you get back," Pike told Bonds. "You and McConnell keep moving along the river and we'll catch up."

"Right," Bonds said. "Come on, men."

He and his men went off on their sad chore and Pike turned back to the two horses he'd chosen for himself and Bridger. As he finished saddling them, McConnell came along with two sacks of supplies.

"You've got enough here for two days each," he said, handing them to Pike. "Hopefully, you won't need that much time."

"If we don't find 'The Bold' in two days we'll turn back and join you."

"Where have I heard that before?" McConnell asked his friend.

Pike had finished tying the sacks to his and Bridger's saddle when Jim Bridger joined them.

"How are they?" Pike asked.

"How could they be?" Bridger asked. "At least one of them has the love and comfort of her children. The other woman is going to be alone for a long time."

Pike studied Bridger's face for a moment and then said, "Did either of them blame you?"

Bridger looked at Pike and said, "No."

"But you blame yourself, don't you?"

"Yeah," Bridger said, "I do—but don't start thinking I'm fallin' apart, okay? If there was one person you had to blame for all of this, who would it be?"

Pike didn't reply.

"Come on," Bridger said, to both him and McConnell, "give me an honest answer."

Finally, Pike said, "Iron Eagle."

Bridger turned to McConnell and said, "Keep the men back from the tributaries. From now on I want everyone to stay together, understand?"

"Sure, Bridger," McConnell said. "Hurry back, huh? I don't know how long I can keep fooling these people into thinking I know what I'm doing."

Bridger smiled and put his hand on McConnell's shoulder.

"As long as you and I believe it, that's all that matters."

Bridger accepted his horse's reins from Pike and mounted up.

"Keep things calm here, Skins," Pike said.

"You keep your eyes open, Pike."

"I will," Pike said. He looked around and said, "Speaking of keeping my eyes open, have you seen Jeanna anywhere?"

"She's with one of the widows," Bridger said. "She was a big help with Mrs. Davidson."

Pike looked down at McConnell and said, "Explain this to Jeanna for me, will you?"

"Oh sure," McConnell said, "now give me something easy to do."

Iron Eagle was very satisfied with what he and his people had accomplished. Sitting at his fire he wondered how the big white man, Pike, was going to react when he found out what the Crow braves had done.

He hoped it would make Pike come looking for him. Iron Eagle would not rest until he had the big white man on the end of his lance, squirming and begging for his life.

"When will we strike next, Iron Eagle?" Great Buffalo asked. "Our braves have tasted the blood of the white man, and thirst for more."

"Soon, Great Buffalo," Iron Eagle said. "Very soon they will taste it again. Very soon there will be a flood of white man's blood to soothe our brother's thirst."

But the blood of the big man, Pike, would be for Iron Eagle, only.

"The Bold" had not seen Iron Eagle in days, and this worried him. There were enough of his young braves missing that he was sure they had left with the hot-headed Iron Eagle.

If Iron Eagle had defied him, if he had gone against the whites—and lived—then he would have "The Bold" to answer to.

The Crow chief could not allow one of his braves to openly defy him, and not pay the price.

With his very life!

Chapter Thirty-two

This was the first time Pike and Bridger had been truly alone since the trouble with the Crow had started. Pike decided that his friend needed talking to, to make sure that this ordeal did not have a lasting effect on him. Jim Bridger was a legend in the mountains, and it was clear to Pike that even a legend can have a chink in his armor—but if the chink went untreated it would widen more and more, until the entire armor fell away.

"Jim, can I ask you something?"

"Why not?" Bridger answered. "We're the only ones here, aren't we?"

"Jesus," Pike said, "I hope so."

Bridger looked at him, allowed himself a small smile, and then faced front again.

"What's the question?" Bridger asked.

"Why did you decide to come out to the Yellowstone with so many people?"

There was a long silence and then Bridger said, "A moment of madness, I guess."

"Seriously."

"You won't accept that as a serious answer?"

"No."

They rode in silence for a while longer, and then Bridger said, "It got out of hand."

"What did?"

"The idea I had," Bridger said.

"Which was what?"

"I thought that a group of trappers and hunters, wintering on the Yellowstone, could do remarkably well for themselves, maybe even come out of the winter as very rich men."

"And?"

"And I started out with a small group—and suddenly it started to grow. Others heard about our excursion and wanted to come along. Then more, and many of them with families that they didn't want to leave behind."

"You could have taken only single hunters," Pike said, "or those who were willing to leave their families."

"Yes, I could have," Bridger said, "and I should have, but I got carried away with the whole thing. I allowed my ego to influence my judgment."

"Ego," Pike said. "I didn't think you had one."

"You know," Bridger said, "I didn't either, but you know what I learned from this farce?"

"What?"

"We all have egos, and we can't afford to let them get the better of us."

"No, I guess not," Pike said. He *knew* he had an ego, and he knew he had let it run away with him once or twice—or more. "I know what you mean."

"How could you?" Bridger said. "You don't have an ego."

"Oh, I have an ego, all right."

"Well, you don't have an ego problem!"

"Once we admit we have egos I think we have to admit the possibility of it becoming a problem."

"I've never seen any hint of an ego in you."

"Men our size, Jim," Pike said, for Bridger was

almost as big as he was, "have to watch our ego more than most."

"Why do you say that?"

"We attract trouble," Pike said. "We attract it from men who want to see if we're as tough as we are big. We attract it from men bigger than we are, or men who think we're bigger than we are. We attract it from women, don't we? Women who want to see if we're big all over?"

Bridger laughed and Pike knew that he'd struck a chord with the remark about women.

"Lord knows I've never had any shortage of willing women," Bridger said. "I guess the same can be said of you, eh?"

"Oh yeah," Pike said, "and look at the two of us. We're still here. We've survived it all. We've even survived confrontations with bears, and we're still here. That has to feed a man's ego, doesn't it?"

"You're right," Bridger said, "but you always seem to keep it in check."

"Well, I have to say I've always thought the same of you."

"Now you know different."

"No, I don't," Pike said. "Any man would doubt himself after what you've been through."

"After what I've been through?" Bridger said. "What about what you went through?"

"That wasn't your fault, for Chrissake," Pike said. "Jesus, Jim, it was my idea to go out there scouting for Crow, and nobody pushed McConnell into going with me."

"What about Candy—"

"Oh, let's not get into that again!" Pike said, being deliberately harsh. "John Candy was a grown man, he knew what he was getting into."

They rode in silence for a time after that, and then Bridger said, "Thanks, Pike."

"For what?"

"For talking to me."

"Hey, it's either talk to you or this horse."

"You know what I mean," Bridger said. "Thanks for wanting to help."

"You're too good a man, Jim, to let this eat away at you."

"I'll try to keep that in mind."

They had ridden most of the first day before stopping to camp. They weren't pushing the horses, or themselves. Essentially, what they were doing was hoping they'd simply run into "The Bold" and his Crow braves, while hoping they wouldn't run into Iron Eagle and his, or the Blackfeet. They were trusting more to chance than anything else, but when you trust to chance you always have to realize that chance usually has a mind of its own.

They had camped and had dinner and set their watches when Bridger, on the first watch, heard something. He woke Pike, with his hand over the bigger man's mouth to keep him from crying out inadvertently.

"What?" Pike said in a whisper after Bridger had moved his hand.

"Something," Bridger said. "I heard something."

They both moved away from the fire in opposite directions, Bridger with his Kentucky pistol in hand, Pike with his borrowed Sharps.

They stayed stock still for more than ten minutes, unable to see each other. They were both disciplined enough, though, not to try to communicate.

Pike hadn't heard anything, but he had a feeling, and that combined with the fact that Bridger had heard something was good enough for him.

He'd stay right where he was until morning, if he had to, and he knew Bridger would do the same thing.

They didn't have to, though.

Pike heard the sound of a horse's hoof on stone, and it was the sound of an unshod horse.

There were Indians nearby — *very* nearby — and now it was only a matter of how many . . . and who.

Pike was careful not to look in the direction of the fire. He did not want to diminish his night vision one iota. He waited, his head cocked, listening for the sound that would tell him that someone was entering their camp.

By now the Indians might have dismounted, so he was listening for a very different sound. Of course, since they were dealing with Indians — Crow or Blackfoot, it didn't much matter which — there was always the chance that he wouldn't hear anything. In that case he and Bridger would have to rely on their instincts.

He wished they had thought of stuffing their blankets so that it looked like they were underneath them, but they hadn't had time for that.

In spite of the cold Pike felt himself beginning to sweat underneath his armpits. He flexed his hands on the Sharps so that they might dry a bit.

Finally, something caught his attention. He wasn't sure whether it was something he heard or felt, but he had chosen a direction and was staring that way when he saw someone step from the darkness into the ring of light their campfire was supplying.

189

It was an Indian, and he felt sure it was a Crow.

He watched the brave, who seemed to have stopped and looked like he was sniffing the air. Finally, the brave waved to someone and was joined on the edge of the light by one, then another, and finally a third Crow brave.

Pike assumed that Bridger had also seen them, but he and Bridger were at opposite ends of the camp, and the Indians had entered at a point almost exactly between them. If they were going to take these braves it was going to have to be quietly, without a shot, so as not to alert any others who might be nearby.

Carefully, he laid the Sharps down on the ground and removed his knife from his belt. He knew that Bridger would be doing the same thing.

Ostensibly, since Bridger was the leader in camp, he had to be considered the leader outside, as well, so Pike resigned himself to waiting for Bridger to make the first move.

So he waited.

Part Six
The Stand

Chapter Thirty-three

Pike watched the darkness opposite him, past the Indians, who were now moving quietly into the camp. Suddenly, he saw one of the braves stiffen, and he knew that they had seen the empty blanket rolls.

At that moment there was a loud shout from across the camp and Jim Bridger came charging out. The braves turned in his direction as he launched himself in a dive at them. Arms outstretched, he struck two of them and bore them down to the ground.

The remaining braves moved toward the three men on the ground, and Pike broke from his cover and ran toward them. Unlike Bridger, he did not shout and let them know that he was coming. When he struck them in the small of the back with his body he felt them fold almost in half, the air going from their lungs. He righted himself quickly and struck one of them on the butt of the jaw with his closed fist, knocking him unconscious. The other brave tried to roll away, but the grimace of pain on his face told Pike that he had done the man some injury, probably to his lower back. He took a step toward the man and kicked him in the side of the head.

Bridger, meanwhile, was not in as advantageous a

position as Pike. He was on the ground with the two braves he had tackled, and the three of them were rolling around, each looking for some purchase. Bridger finally found his knees and launched a punch from that position. He felt his fist connect with someone's throat and there was a strangling sound as one of the braves suddenly could not breathe.

The second brave drew his knife and swiped at Bridger with it, but the man was off balance and fell well short. Bridger, not wanting to kill the man, reversed his knife and struck the man a blow on the forehead. The man slumped to the hard, cold ground and did not move.

Bridger stayed on his knees a moment, catching his breath, and then Pike stepped to him and helped him to his feet.

"Did we kill any of them?" Bridger asked.

"No," Pike said, "which is good, because they might be 'The Bold's' men."

"What were they doing sneaking into our camp, then?" Bridger asked.

"Why don't we tie them up and ask them?" Pike suggested.

When the first brave roused himself and found that he was bound he fought against the ropes until he had exhausted himself. Pike and Bridger sat across the fire from him, drinking coffee, watching him.

"What do you think?" Bridger asked.

"Let's wait until they're all awake," Pike said. "We don't know which one is going to talk, so we might as well ask all of them at the same time."

They waited and, one by one, the braves regained consciousness. To a man they all struggled against their bonds until they had to stop to catch their breath.

"Who sent you?" Pike asked, first in English, and then in halting Crow.

There was no answer.

Pike leaned forward and picked a burning stick of wood from the fire. He held it out in front of him, hoping that the braves would grasp his meaning.

"Who sent you?" he asked again. "Who do you ride with?"

They didn't answer, but he had caught their attention with the burning piece of wood.

"Iron Eagle?" Pike asked.

" 'The Bold'?" Bridger asked.

Pike decided to try a hunch. It would either work, or they'd get so mad they'd never talk.

"Do you ride with the Blackfeet?"

Two of the braves glared at him, one spat, and the fourth man spoke.

"We are Crow," he said. "We kill Blackfeet dogs."

"Well," Pike said, "this is a step in the right direction."

Bridger nodded and Pike dropped the burning wood back into the fire.

"What is your name?" he asked the brave who had spoken.

"Two Moons."

"Well, Two Moons, if you don't ride with the Blackfeet, who do you ride with?"

"I follow my chief," Two Moons said proudly.

" 'The Bold'?"

Two Moons nodded.

"We have a truce with 'The Bold'," Pike said.

"Why do you sneak into our camp?"

"You are *Casapy?*" Two Moons asked Pike.

"I am *Casapy,*" Bridger said.

"We did not know," the man said, and from the stricken look on his face Pike and Bridger believed him. "We would not willingly defy the word of our chief."

"I believe you, Two Moons."

Pike exchanged a glance with Bridger, who nodded. They both moved to the Indians and untied them all.

"We regret any injury we may have caused you," Pike said. "Please, share our food and in the morning we would like you to take us to 'The Bold'."

"So you can tell him of our folly?" Two Moons asked, rubbing his wrists.

"No," Pike said, "he will not be told by us. We must speak to him of Iron Eagle, who has deliberately broken 'The Bold's' truce by killing five of our men."

The braves looked at each other, and then at the meat Pike and Bridger had put on the fire.

"Very well," Two Moons said. "We will take you."

"Let me cut you some meat," Pike said, taking out his knife. "You all look hungry."

Pike and Bridger took turns keeping watch that night, and noticed that one of the braves was also always awake. In the morning they all rose together. Pike and Bridger saddled their horses, and then they walked to where the braves had left their horses. Once they were all mounted Pike and Bridger simply followed the Crow braves. They realized that they might be walking into a trap, that these braves might be leading them to Iron Eagle instead of 'The Bold', but chose to believe that the braves were sincere.

They agreed on this, and if they were going to be mistaken and end up getting killed, they figured they might as well be in agreement.

Chapter Thirty-four

When they reached the Crow camp Pike breathed a sigh of relief. It was obviously "The Bold's" camp, as there were women and children in view. He doubted that Iron Eagle would have taken women and children with him.

As had happened before, they were the center of attention as they rode through the camp, some of the children running alongside of them, taking a good look at their white skin and beards.

When they dismounted Two Moons had one of the other braves take their horses and said, "This way."

They followed him to a lodge, where he halted them with a wave of his hand and went inside. While they waited they were ringed by curious children and Pike even picked one up and put him on his shoulders. The little boy, barely five, squealed with delight at being so high up in the air.

Two Moons came out of the lodge and said, "He will see you now."

Pike put the child down gently and stepped into the lodge first, followed by Bridger.

"Casapy," "The Bold" said, "you honor me."

"I am also honored that you agreed to see us," Bridger said.

"Sit by my fire," "The Bold" invited, and they sat

opposite him.

"Two Moons told me of his blunder," "The Bold" said. "I thank you for not killing any of my men."

"Did he also tell you why we wished to speak with you?" Bridger asked.

"No."

"It is Iron Eagle," Bridger said. "We believe he attacked and tortured and killed five of our people, mutilating them in a manner which was useless."

The old chief frowned, adding more lines to an already deeply lined face. "You saw Iron Eagle do this thing?"

"No," Bridger said, "but—"

"Then why do you accuse him?" "The Bold" asked. "It is very serious to accuse him of breaking my word."

"Please," Pike said, leaning forward, "let us not pretend. We all know what a hothead Iron Eagle is. I can't believe that he agreed so readily to uphold this truce between us—did he?"

"The Bold" regarded them both for a long moment, then shook his head.

"No," he said, finally, "he did not. I have been worried that he would do a thing such as you have described."

"Do you know where he is?" Pike asked.

"I do not," "The Bold" said.

"Can you find him?"

"The Bold" hesitated, then nodded.

"When I do," he said, "I will ask if he did as you accuse."

"He will deny it," Bridger said.

"If he does," "The Bold" said, "I will know, anyway. Once I have satisfied myself of his guilt, I will deal with him."

"If he comes after any of my people again," Bridger said, "I will kill him, and those who follow him. I do not want this to be looked upon as our breaking the truce."

"It will not," "The Bold" assured them. "You will do what you must to protect your people. I understand that."

"We appreciate your understanding," Bridger said. "You are a great chief."

Grimly, "The Bold" said, "If I was a great chief, I would not be defied by one of my braves."

They didn't know what to say to that.

"Will you stay with us?" "The Bold" asked. "I will have Two Moons see to your comfort."

"If it will not offend you," Bridger said, "we would like to get back to our people as soon as possible."

"I understand," "The Bold" said. "Two Moons will give you whatever you need to make your trip easier. Fresh horses, supplies—"

"We have all we need," Bridger said, and he and Pike stood up. "Again, we thank you for your understanding of this matter."

"I have given you my word," "The Bold" said, his eyes cold, narrow slits. "Those who have broken it will pay dearly."

Looking into the older man's face, Pike had no doubt of that.

He was also glad that it was not he who had broken the chief's word.

They had stepped outside the lodge when something occurred to Pike.

"Wait a minute," Pike said to Bridger. "I've got an idea."

Skins McConnell was worried.

He wasn't so much worried about Pike and Bridger. He knew they could take care of themselves. He was worried about himself, and about the people who had been left in his charge.

After Pike and Bridger had left, McConnell waited for Bonds and his men to return with the bodies. Afterward they chipped through the ice of the Yellowstone and dropped the blanket wrapped bodies into the cold water beneath. McConnell said some words from the Bible, and then they moved on.

"What's wrong?" Bonds asked, riding alongside McConnell.

"Why do you ask?"

"You've a mighty worried look on your face," Barry Bonds said. "You're not very good at hiding it."

"Do you hear it?" McConnell asked.

"Hear what?"

"That's what I mean?" McConnell said. "I don't hear anything."

"It's winter," Bonds said. "The birds have gone, the bears are hibernating, the critters are trying to keep warm—"

"I don't care," McConnell said. "You can usually hear some kind of noise if you listen hard enough. A wolf, a deer, a buffalo, something."

They rode in silence, both listening.

"I don't hear a thing," Bonds said, finally.

"I know," McConnell said, "and that's what's got me so worried."

Bonds listened again, so intently that he screwed up his face.

Finally he said, "I'll want the others to be on the

alert."

"You do that," McConnell said.

He hoped that whatever was out there, watching them, that it would turn out to be Iron Eagle and his handful of braves. At least they wouldn't be so foolish as to come charging down at them when they were so outnumbered.

The Blackfeet, however, were another story.

Iron Eagle looked down at the whites who were moving along the river. There were a lot of them, too many for he and his braves to attack openly. He was annoyed, though, that they were all staying together, sending no one out along the tributaries to trap and hunt so that Iron Eagle and his braves could pick them off.

"This is useless," Great Buffalo said. "If they stay together there is nothing we can do."

Iron Eagle looked at Great Buffalo, who had followed him without question since they were children together. If even Great Buffalo was having second thoughts now, what of the other twenty or so braves he had with him?

Iron Eagle was just about to decide on a drastic course of action when he heard something from behind.

Barry Bonds came riding up on Skins McConnell again. McConnell had already called their motion to a halt.

"I hear something," he said.

"Yeah," McConnell said, "so do I."

They both sat and listened and heard it again.

They looked at each other, but neither of them had to say a word. They knew what they were hearing, and the sound wasn't all that far off.

Shots.

Pike and Bridger reined in when they heard the shots.

"Shit," Bridger said.

"Take it easy," Pike said. "There's nothing we can do from here."

"Well then let's get there," Bridger said, and kicked his horse in the ribs, shooting ahead of Pike.

Pike hoped the rest of them would be able to keep up.

"What do we do?" Bonds asked. "Make a run for it?"

"We can't," McConnell said. "Not with all of the people we have, and the pack animals. Besides, where the hell would we run to?"

Bonds looked back and saw the rest of their people. Some of them were watching he and Mc-Connell, others had their heads cocked, listening to the sounds of shots in the not so distant distance.

"If we're gonna do something we'd better do it fast," he said.

"We'll have to hole up," McConnell said, "find some cover and wait."

"Wait for what?"

"For whatever's coming," McConnell said. "Let's get to it."

Chapter Thirty-five

When Pike caught up to Bridger he found him sitting his horse among a group of bodies, looking down at them. Pike slowed his horse and rode in among the bodies himself, looking at their dead faces.

"Jesus," he said when he found a familiar one. "They look like they never had a chance."

"Outnumbered," Bridger said. "Looks like they were taken from behind."

Pike stopped his horses and stepped down. As he did the Crow braves that "The Bold" had given them caught up to them and also walked their horses in among the carnage.

Pike crouched down over Iron Eagle to check him and make sure he was dead. The hotheaded Crow had paid dearly for defying his chief. There were at least four or five bullet holes in him.

The Crow were moving among the bodies, and around the perimeter.

Two Moons dismounted and came up next to Pike, also looking down at Iron Eagle.

"Blackfeet," Two Moons said.

"I figured that," Pike said. He stood up and said to Two Moons, "How many?"

"A hundred," Two Moons said, with a shrug, which meant more or less.

"Pike," Bridger said, an edge to his voice.

"I know, Jim," Pike said. He turned to Two Moons and said, "Are you prepared to go against the Blackfoot?"

"My chief said to do whatever we must to help you," Two Moons said.

"All right," Pike said. "Tell your men to be ready."

Two Moons went back to his horse and Pike mounted his and looked at Bridger, who was sitting his horse stiffly next to him.

"I don't hear anything, yet," Bridger said.

"Well, let's hope we get there in time," Pike said.

They had found some cover along a curve in the riverbank. There were some large boulders, some ground depressions. It wasn't much, but McConnell knew it would have to do.

"We'll have to spread out along here," he called out to Bonds and anyone else who was listening.

"We're out in the open," Jeb Kane complained.

"We'll have to get down low," McConnell said, "but we've got some cover here."

"What about the women and children?" Jeb asked.

McConnell thought a moment before replying.

"I'd hate to have to mule fort," he said. That meant slitting the throats of all the mules they had and using the carcasses for cover.

"We need those mules," Jeb Kane said. "Without them to carry our skins we've wasted the winter."

"Jeb," Barry Bonds said, "if we're all dead the skins won't matter, will they?"

"Jesus . . ." Kane said, but he knew they were right.

"How many mules do we have?" McConnell asked.

"Close to forty," Bonds said, "and over a hundred horses."

"I don't want to kill the horses," McConnell said.

"Doesn't the same logic apply to the horses that applies to the mules?" Kane asked.

"We may come to a point where we'll want to send the women and children ahead while we try to hold the Blackfeet off," McConnell said.

"Or Crow," Bonds said.

"I don't think so," McConnell said. "Anyway, kill about twenty mules and use them for cover for the women and children."

"What about the horses?" Kane asked.

"What about them?"

"They'll be out in the open," he said.

"We can't create any cover for them," McConnell said. "Every man will have to care for his own horse."

"What are you going to do?" Kane asked.

"I'm gonna lay mine down, use it for cover and hope it doesn't get hit by the stray bullet."

"That's craz—" Kane started, but he was silenced by Barry Bonds.

"Look!" Bonds cried out.

He was pointing and they looked in that direction. There were several Indians—Blackfeet, McConnell was sure—sitting their horses, watching them.

"Scouts," McConnell said. "The main party will be here soon. Let's get busy making that cover."

"I don't know if we're going to get out of this one," Bonds said before he ran down the line, shouting orders.

"Yeah," McConnell said, squinting at the Indians. He hoped that Pike and Bridger were a long way off, because if they heard the commotion he knew they'd come riding right into it.

It was deadly quiet.

It was an amazing sight. There were animals lying all along the river bank, some of them alive and some of them dead. Behind the animals crouched men, women and children, waiting, some of them calm, some in panic.

There were men crouched behind rocks and lying in basin-like depressions, some of which were filled with thin ice that broke beneath them, causing them to be lying in cold water.

McConnell was crouched behind his horse, glad that he wasn't the kind of idiot who got close to his animal and named them. You never knew when you were going to have to eat your horse, or use it for cover. Giving the animal a name would make that hard to do.

He had a young man with him, one of those he and Pike had taught to load. In fact, each armed man had someone behind cover with him to load for him. They had gathered together all the weapons they had in camp, and most of the men had two or three guns. Once they fired one they'd hand it to their helper, who would reload it while the man fired the other weapon.

Barry Bonds was also lying behind his horse, some ten yards farther along the bank. McConnell had suggested that they put some distance between them. If the people survived the charge that was to come, they'd need one of them—McConnell or Bonds—to get them moving again.

Despite the cold McConnell felt himself sweating.

It was soaking his armpits, which felt like they were freezing as the cold air found the moist patches.

Jeb Kane was lying behind a boulder near McConnell. His horse was standing off to one side. Kane had been unable to keep the horse down. The same had happened with some of the other men, and their horses had wandered off. Those animals would have to be caught if there was any need for them later.

"Where the hell are they?" Kane called out to McConnell.

"They want us to worry," McConnell said, "to think about what's going to happen."

"Well, they're gettin' their wish."

"Let's keep it quiet, Kane," McConnell said.

"What the hell for?" Kane said, but lapsed into silence nonetheless.

McConnell scanned the ridge just above them, where they had seen the scouts. Some of the Indians would come from there, but he was sure they'd spread out before they charged. He only hoped that none of them had worked their way across the river further down. If that happened they'd be attacked from behind, as well, and if that happened they'd be defenseless.

The river looked some shallow here and he wondered if the ice would even hold the weight of a man or a horse—or both.

"Mr. McConnell?" the boy next to him asked.

"Yeah, boy?"

"Will they have guns?" he asked. "I mean, the Indians, when they come, will they have guns?"

McConnell looked at the boy.

"Some of them will, yeah, but most of them will have bows and arrows. You see, the Indians are impressed by our weapons, but the guns are useless during a charge. Once they fire them they can't stop to reload, so from that point on they're only as good as a club. With the bow and arrow they can keep firing at us as they charge."

"I see."

McConnell looked back up at the ridge.

"Are we gonna live through this, Mr. McConnell?"

McConnell looked at the boy again. He guessed he was probably about fourteen. His name was Tommy something, he couldn't remember the last name.

"You just be ready to load, Tommy," McConnell said.

"It's not me I'm worried about," Tommy somebody said. "It's my mother and sister."

McConnell stared at him a moment.

"How old is your sister?"

"Thirteen."

McConnell guessed his mother would be in her mid-thirties or so.

"Tommy, if things get real bad I'm gonna tell you to get out."

"Get out. How—"

"You'll grab a horse and get your mother and sister on it and start them riding. After you've done that you'll find an animal for yourself and take off after them."

"And leave you here?"

"To cover for you," McConnell said. "If it comes to that most of us will cover while the women and children run for it. With a little luck we'll be able to hold them off long enough for you to reach Clark's Fork. There's a settlement near there—"

"Mr. McConnell—"

"You call me Skins, boy," McConnell said, "and you do what I tell you, you hear?"

"I hear you, sir—er, Skins."

McConnell looked up and saw movement on the ridge.

"You sure you remember how to load, boy?"

"I think so, sir."

"You'd better know, boy," McConnell said, "because here come those sons of bitches now!"

When the shots came Bridger looked over at Pike.

"That's it," Bridger said.

Pike reached out and put his hand on his friend's arm.

"You push that horse too fast he's gonna step into a hole or something and break a leg," he said. "They're not helpless. They should be able to hold them off until we get there."

"I hope so," Bridger said.

They had been moving along at a steady, not-too-fast pace. Pike stopped his horse and turned to wait for Two Moons to catch up to them.

"I hear it," Two Moons said.

"Are you and your braves ready to go up against a hundred Blackfeet?"

Two Moons smiled.

"Twenty-five Crow, a hundred Blackfeet," he said. "That sounds right to me."

Pike looked at the worried Bridger and said, "Sounds like the river. Let's get there."

When Pike, Bridger and the Crow reached the river the separate factions were well into the battle. Pike could see the actions that the whites had taken, and had no doubt that the ideas had come from McConnell. From what he could see his friend had done everything he could, and the campers were fighting valiantly against the charging Blackfeet.

"Jesus," Bridger said.

"Let's get down there and help them," Pike said. "What do you say?"

Bridger looked at him and said, "I think it's time to do it."

They both looked at Two Moons, who nodded his agreement.

"That is why we are here."

Pike, Bridger and the twenty-five Crow charged down toward the battle, hoping that their surprise attack from behind the Blackfeet would have some effect—maybe even rout them.

Fat chance, Pike thought, but maybe we can just do some damage and let them know they're in a fight.

McConnell couldn't believe his eyes. As if they didn't have enough trouble, there were more of them coming down towards them.

Suddenly he recognized Pike, and then Bridger, and realized that they had come to the rescue with Crow braves at their side.

"All right!" he shouted.

He could see that there were only twenty or twenty-five Crow braves with them, but still they were attacking from behind. The element of surprise was with them, and he could only hope they'd make the most of it.

"Skins—" Tommy said, puzzled.

"Just keep loading, boy!" McConnell said, handing him his empty weapon and accepting a freshly loaded one. "We got us some help."

Chapter Thirty-six

Pike fired his Sharps first and then reached for the Kentucky pistol he had taken with him from camp. Even as a Blackfoot brave was falling from his horse with Pike's ball in his back, Pike lined up his second shot and fired, knocking another brave to the ground.

Having fired both weapons he tucked the pistol back into his belt and then reversed the Sharps, so he could swing it as a club. He rode into the midst of the Blackfeet, who had finally realized that something was happening from behind them, and began sweeping them from their horses right and left.

Charging down toward the Blackfeet, Pike had been able to hear the war cries of the Crow, but now that he was in the midst of the battle he couldn't tell the Crow cries from those of the Blackfeet.

He lost track of Bridger, but assumed that he would be acquitting himself well.

He turned to strike a Blackfoot brave from behind and suddenly *he* was hit from behind and taken from his saddle.

McConnell watched as the Blackfeet tried to decide whether to charge straight at them or semicircle them, trying to hem them in between themselves and the river behind them.

He grabbed his weapons from Tommy and fired, trying to make sure every shot counted. He passed the boy the spent weapon, grabbed a loaded one, lined up his shot and fired again.

He wondered when the Blackfeet would realize they were being attacked from behind, and at that moment he saw the Crow ride into the midst of their enemies.

He knew Pike and Bridger were in there, too, and saw the charge of the Blackfeet stall just a bit. They were confused, and it would be a few heated moments before they realized what was happening.

McConnell stood up and shouted, "We're getting some help! Let's give them a hand!"

He charged from cover, his horse rising up behind him. He grabbed the horse's reins and was about to mount the animal when he saw that it was bleeding from its left flank. He released the animal then, took up his loaded rifle and charged the Blackfeet on foot. Barry Bonds saw what McConnell was doing and stood up to follow.

There was some hesitancy on the part of the other men, but soon they, too, were charging forward, some on foot, some on horseback.

Tommy had a loaded rifle in his hand, stood up and decided to follow McConnell into battle. As he took his first step an arrow struck him in the chest, knocking him over backward.

As he stared at the sky he wondered about his mother and sister.

Pike struck the ground hard with a weight on his

back. Although the air rushed from his lungs he knew he couldn't take the time to try and regain it. He rolled, pushed away from the weight behind him, kicking at the Blackfoot brave as he drew his knife. The brave regained his balance and sprang at Pike, who brought the knife up to meet him, impaling the brave on the blade. The Indian's warm blood flowed over his hand, and he pushed the dead man onto his back and pulled the knife free. As he stood up, a mounted Blackfoot brave rode toward him and he reached up to defend himself. As the brave approached him he staggered and fell from his horse. Pike looked around and saw Jim Bridger standing on his feet, blood staining his forehead. Bridger had fired at the brave before he could take Pike's head off, and Pike waved his thanks.

He lost track of Bridger again after that. He picked up his rifle and once again began using it as a club. He felt something strike his left arm, but didn't let it slow him down.

"Pike!"

He knew the voice well and turned to find Skins McConnell running toward him, grinning broadly despite that fact that there was some blood on his left shoulder.

"What the hell are you doing out here?" Pike demanded.

"Saving your ass!" McConnell said.

"Jesus, you ass—" Pike started, but they both turned to face two braves who were charging them on foot. They dispatched the Indians with their rifles, clubbing them down, and then stood back to back, looking for more.

But there was no more coming.

"What's happening?" McConnell said.

"They're turning tail!" Pike shouted.

Sure enough, the Blackfeet were charging back up to the ridge, and the white men and the Crow were so pleased to see them go that they didn't bother to chase them.

Bridger came over and stood with Pike and McConnell, watching the Blackfeet retreat.

"We confused the hell out of them," he said.

"They'll take some time to regroup," Pike said. "We'll have to get out of here before that."

He turned around and looked down at the riverbank, where many of the whites were waving and cheering.

He looked at McConnell and said, "Who the hell killed all the mules?"

McConnell stared at his friend and said, "How about introducing me to your friends?"

Epilogue

Pike stared up at Jeanna, who was seated astride him with his erection trapped between them. She leaned over to dangle her full breasts in his face, and he nipped at her nipples while she squealed in delight.

He took hold of her buttocks, raised her off him enough to free his erection, and then lowered her onto him until he was buried deep inside of her.

She sat up straight and arched her back, riding him up and down while he held her buttocks. His feet were flat down on the bed and she reached behind her to brace a hand on each knee and moved on him in longer, slower strokes. Pike let her work at her own tempo and before long she was bouncing up and down on him faster and faster, her breath coming in long, ragged gasps. When he finally exploded inside of her she had lay down on him, her breasts flattened against his chest, her teeth in his shoulder . . .

After Pike, Bridger, and the Crow had broken the attack of the Blackfoot Indians they had quickly seen to their wounded and dead, recaptured the horses who had strayed away and taken count of the animals they had lost. Using the animals they had left they took only what was essential and, accompanied by the Crow braves, made their way to Clark's Fork.

When they reached that point the Crow went back and Pike, Bridger and his people went on to the Clark's Fork settlement. There they would decide who would stay together and who would go their own way. Bridger had decided that anyone who wanted to see the winter through with him was welcome to stay with him. Pike was pleased to see that, and it looked as if half of the people were willing to do that. The other half had had enough of wintering on the Yellowstone, and were planning to go their own ways. Some of them would even stay at the settlement until winter was over.

Pike and McConnell planned to spend a few days at the Clark's Fork settlement. They were both friends with Ted Clark, who ran the trading post, who insisted they stay at least that long.

Pike didn't know what Jeanna was going to do, but he spent those few days with her in a tent on the edge of the settlement, saying goodbye. He hoped that McConnell was saying his successful goodbyes to Donna, as well.

The day Pike was ready to depart he left Jeanna asleep in the tent. When she woke he hoped that she wouldn't cry—at least, not tears of sadness.

He found McConnell waiting for him in front of the Trading Post with Ted Clark and Clark's Crow wife, Sky Woman.

"I've got whatever supplies we need," McConnell said.

"Where are you fellas headed?" Clark asked.

"Up," Pike said, "where we won't run into anyone for a long time—we hope." Pike turned to McConnell and asked, "How's Donna?"

"She's all right," McConnell replied. "She understands."

"And your woman?" Sky Woman asked Pike. "She understands?"

"Of course," Pike said. "She's a Crow woman."

Sky Woman could not argue with him after that. "You need a woman, Jack Pike," was all he could say.

"Well, when you're ready to leave this bear of a man, you let me know."

"Hah!" Clark said, winding a thick arm around his wife's waist, "never!"

"Where's Bridger?" Pike asked McConnell.

"He's inside," Clark asked. "He's stocking up on supplies. He'll be leaving tomorrow."

"Give me a minute," Pike said to McConnell, who nodded.

Pike went inside the trading post and found Bridger going over the shelves.

"I have something for you," Pike said.

Bridger turned quickly and smiled.

"Here," Pike said, returning the Sharps rifle.

"No, you keep it," Bridger said, waving his hand.

"I got one from Ted Clark," Pike said. "This was a loan, and I want to return it. Who knows when I'll have to borrow it again?"

Bridger hesitated a moment, then nodded and accepted it.

"Leaving?" he asked.

"Now, as a matter of fact," Pike said.

Bridger stuck out his hand.

"I appreciate everything you did, Pike," he said as

219

they shook hands. "More than you know."

"I'm glad everything turned out — well —," he said, as he recalled that Bridger had lost nine people at the riverbank. "— it could have been worse."

"A lot worse," Bridger said, "and thanks to you and Skins, it didn't."

"Good-bye, Jim," Pike said. He started for the door, then turned and said, "Do us both a favor, huh?"

"What's that?"

"Have a quiet rest of the winter."

THE DESTROYER
By Warren Murphy and Richard Sapir

EDGE by George G. Gilman

#5 BLOOD ON SILVER (17-225, $3.50)
The Comstock Lode was one of the richest silver strikes the world had ever seen. So Edge was there. So was the Tabor gang—sadistic killers led by a renegade Quaker. The voluptuous Adele Firman, a band of brutal Shoshone Indians, and an African giant were there, too. Too bad. They learned that gold may be warm but silver is death. They didn't live to forget Edge.

#6 RED RIVER (17-226, $3.50)
In jail for a killing he didn't commit, Edge is puzzled by the prisoner in the next cell. Where had they met before? Was it at Shiloh, or in the horror of Andersonville?

This is the sequel to KILLER'S BREED, an earlier volume in this series. We revisit the bloody days of the Civil War and incredible scenes of cruelty and violence as our young nation splits wide open, blue armies versus gray armies, tainting the land with a river of blood. And Edge was there.

Available wherever paperbacks are sold, or order direct from the Publisher. Send cover price plus 50¢ per copy for mailing and handling to Pinnacle Books, Dept.17-282, 475 Park Avenue South, New York, N.Y. 10016. Residents of New York, New Jersey and Pennsylvania must include sales tax. DO NOT SEND CASH.

WARBOTS by G. Harry Stine

#5 OPERATION HIGH DRAGON   (17-159, $3.95)

Civilization is under attack! A "virus program" has been injected into America's polar-orbit military satellites by an unknown enemy. The only motive can be the preparation for attack against the free world. The source of "infection" is traced to a barren, storm-swept rock-pile in the southern Indian Ocean. Now, it is up to the forces of freedom to search out and destroy the enemy. With the aid of their robot infantry—the Warbots—the Washington Greys mount Operation High Dragon in a climactic battle for the future of the free world.

#6 THE LOST BATTALION   (17-205, $3.95)

Major Curt Carson has his orders to lead his Warbot-equipped Washington Greys in a search-and-destroy mission in the mountain jungles of Borneo. The enemy: a strongly entrenched army of Shiite Muslim guerrillas who have captured the Second Tactical Battalion, threatening them with slaughter. As allies, the Washington Greys have enlisted the Grey Lotus Battalion, a mixed-breed horde of Japanese jungle fighters. Together with their newfound allies, the small band must face swarming hordes of fanatical Shiite guerrillas in a battle that will decide the fate of Southeast Asia and the security of the free world.

#7 OPERATION IRON FIST   (17-253, $3.95)

Russia's centuries-old ambition to conquer lands along its southern border erupts in a savage show of force that pits a horde of Soviet-backed Turkish guerrillas against the freedom-loving Kurds in their homeland high in the Caucasus Mountains. At stake: the rich oil fields of the Middle East. Facing certain annihilation, the valiant Kurds turn to the robot infantry of Major Curt Carson's "Ghost Forces" for help. But the brutal Turks far outnumber Carson's desperately embattled Washington Greys, and on the blood-stained slopes of historic Mount Ararat, the hightech warriors of tomorrow must face their most awesome challenge yet!